MAP & MAZE PUZZLES

Sarah Dixon

Illustrated by
Radhi Parekh

Puzzle Contributor: Tim Preston

Contents

Series Editor: Gaby Waters

Puzzle checkers: Harriet Castor and Christina Hopkinson

You will need a pencil, an eraser and some sheets of tracing paper to tackle the puzzles on the pages ahead.

Before You Start

Treasure charts, classic labyrinths, old plans, coded maps ... all these and more lie in wait on the pages ahead. Some of the puzzles are moderately tricky, while others could prove fiendishly difficult. But watch out – it may not be obvious which are which.

To solve the puzzles, look carefully at the illustrations and read the documents thoroughly. It won't be easy. Some of the diaries and letters may be written in strange scripts with odd spellings – but, once deciphered, they could contain vital information. Sometimes you may need to crack a code or figure out a brainteaser before you can even begin to find the answer.

Should you need any help – and you may – there are clues on page 42 to point you in the right direction. And if you are finally stumped, turn to pages 43-48 to find the answers with detailed explanations.

You can pick out a puzzle at random to solve, if you dare. But if you start at the beginning and tackle them in order, you will discover several stories emerging, with a recurring cast of characters. To make sense of these, read on ...

Zoonal Duo and the Mission to Save Quirk

Zoonal Duo is a two-headed troubleshooter from the Ninth Universe. In the space-year 9992 the rulers of the Planet Zarka are planning to transform the Ninth Universe into a giant labyrinth of spaceways. But one planet stands in their way – Quirk, the cradle of civilization. Zoonal's mission is to save Quirk from destruction and thus rescue the Ninth Universe from a labyrinthine fate. The contents of a time capsule which mysteriously appeared in Quirk's southern hemisphere chart Zoonal's journey across space . . . and time.

Hercula and the Five Mighty Feats

Hercula is the local heroine of Harmonika, an island off the coast of Mythika and the heart of one of Quirk's ancient civilizations. Thousands of years ago, the Mythikan Deities decreed that whoever could perform their five tricky tasks would win the Golden Ladle of Heroism. Hercula's bid for this ultimate prize is the subject of five frescoes, discovered by amateur archaeologist Milo Midnight on Harmonika a few years ago.

Sir Gelfrid and Hildegarde and the Singing Rock

Sir Gelfrid and his apprentice knight, Hildegarde, live in the beleaguered kingdom of Loen during Quirk's Dark Age of the Seven Kingdoms. The valiant duo are searching for the Singing Rock which, legend says, will restore joy to Loen. Their adventures are told using a series of illustrations from Dark Age manuscripts.

Waldo Widget and the Search for El Taco

Waldo Widget is a Twystian from the Golden Age of the Seven Kingdoms. He has been a courtier at the palace of Queen Pompadora but then dares to criticize her pet goose, Gosric. The furious queen promptly announces that Waldo is banished from Twystia for life unless he finds the legendary city of El Taco in the recently-discovered land of Terra Nova and sails back with ship-loads of gold. Waldo's travels are illustrated with maps and ancient diaries, now in the museums of Tukan and of Twystia City.

Agent Mistral and the Elite Gang

Four hundred years later, during the Great Gang Era, Terra Nova's Secret Service sends Waldo's descendant, Agent Mistral, to Twystia. Her mission is to investigate the sinister activities of the Elite Gang and its leader, Lucasta Bombasta. Details of this top-secret operation have been pieced together using Mistral's maps and papers, until recently locked in the vaults of the Secret Service HQ.

The Quest

There's more to these five tales than meets the eye, for lying hidden in their midst is a strange story of a stone with legendary powers, now lost in the mists of time. If you keep your eyes open, you can unravel its tangled history. But remember, as centuries pass, it is not only names that can change their form. On page 48, there are hints to lead you on the trail of the stone. But the solution to the central mystery – the location of the lost stone – lies elsewhere in the book for you to find.

The Ancient Star Chart

The Zarkans are preparing to destroy the Planet Quirk in the first phase of their masterplan to build the giant labyrinth of spaceways across the Ninth Universe. The Zarkans' weapon of destruction is the D Ray which can only be neutralized by the Crystal of Leyheyhey. This magical crystal is hidden on one of the 35 stars of the constellation known as the Warp of Arg. In his bid to save Quirk, alien adventurer Zoonal Duo must find the crystal by searching every star in the Warp. But first he has to plot a course along its starways using this ancient star chart.

What is Zoonal's route?

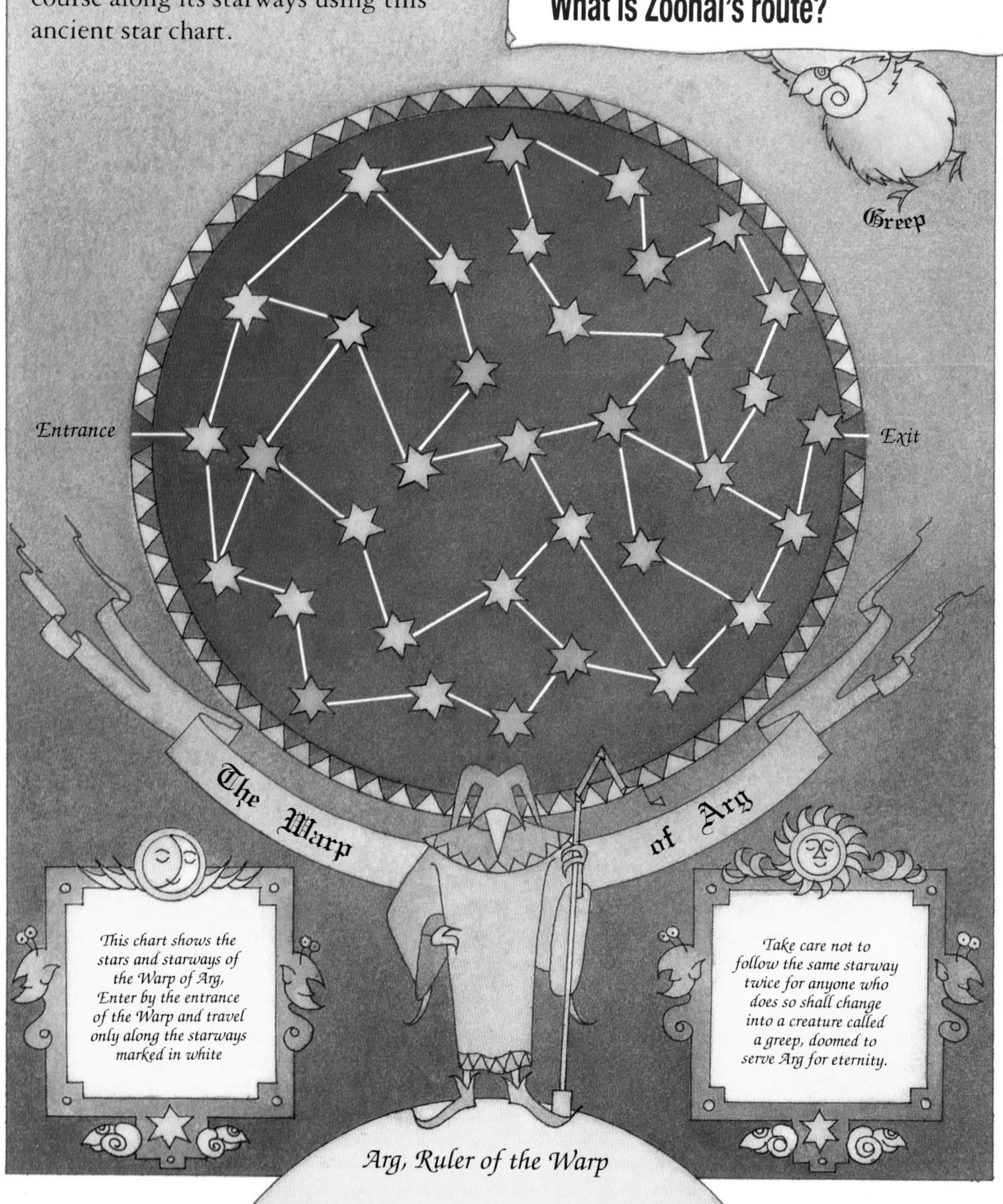

The Labyrinth of Ouzo

For the first of her five feats, Harmonika's local heroine Hercula must free Thrumos, musician to the god Malinger, from the Labyrinth of Ouzo the three-headed satyr. For five long months, Thrumos has been forced to play melodies to soothe Ouzo's triple monster headache, caused by eating the Giant Chocolate Cake of the goddess Migraine. Hercula has Malinger's plan of the labyrinth, depicted on this Harmonikan fresco, to help her find the way. Each matching pair of dots marks the entrance and exit of one of Ouzo's five secret tunnels which run between different sections of his maze. The tunnels themselves are not shown on the plan.

What is Hercula's route?

Balonius's Map

Twystian courtier Waldo Widget arrives in the distant land of Terra Nova, knowing he can only return home if he finds the legendary city of El Taco. His only guide is this map, compass and diary of Balonius the Explorer, the first Twystian to set foot in Terra Nova a hundred years before.

Where is El Taco?

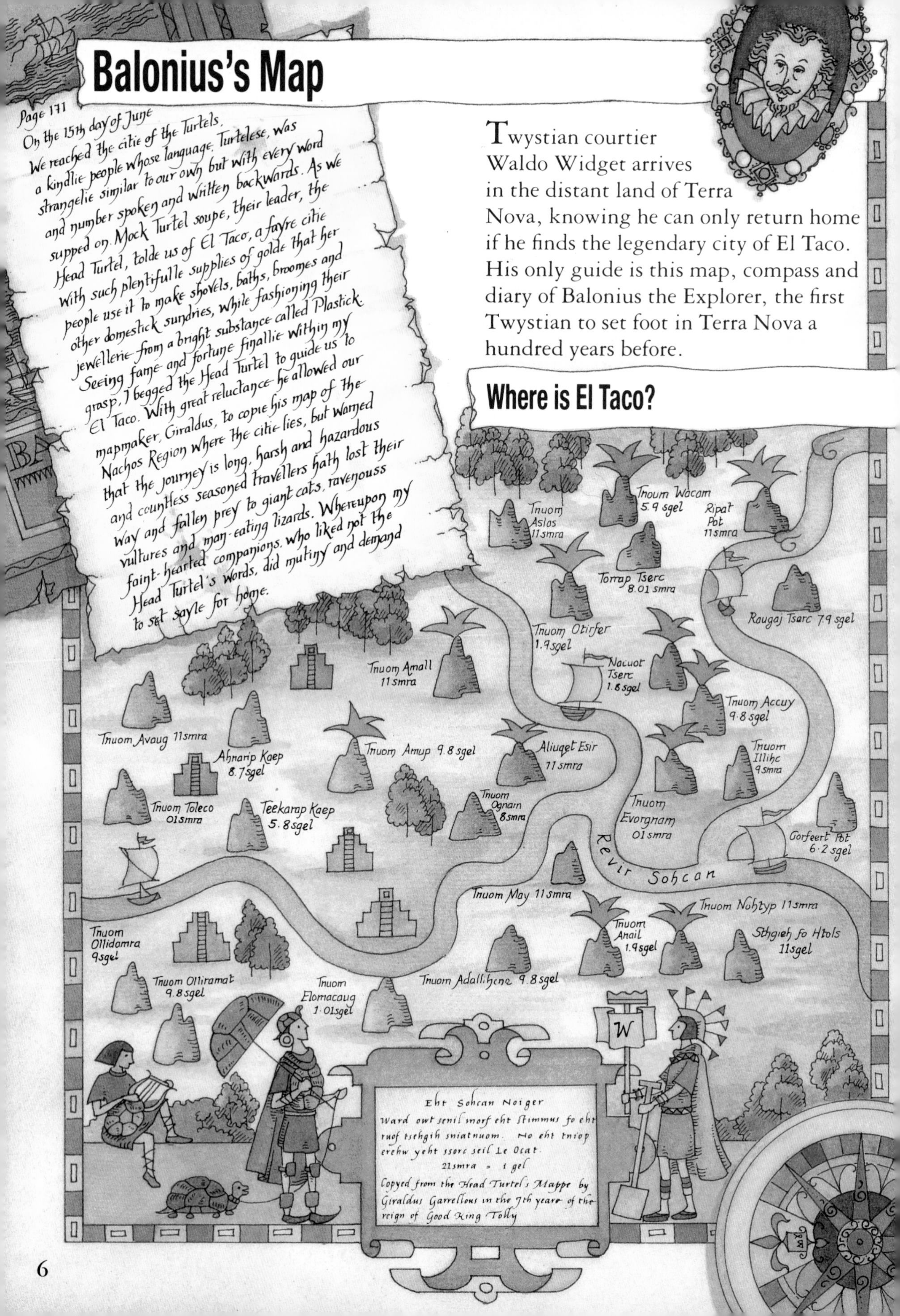

Mappa Blundi

Sir Gelfrid and his apprentice knight, Hildegarde, ride out from the land of Loen in search of the Singing Rock of Lollo Rosso. Unfortunately neither of them know where Lollo Rosso is. By chance they reach the city of Twystia, home of the Mappa Blundi. This famous map depicts all seven cities of the seven kingdoms of the Dark Age world, but the duo must unravel the cryptic clues below the map to discover which city is which.

Which is the city of Lollo Rosso?

The Metro Map

Dispatched to the distant land of Twystia to investigate the shady activities of the Elite Gang, Terra Novan secret agent Mistral has to make contact with a fellow agent at a station on Twystia City's metro system. All the bewildered agent has to go on is a cryptic telegram, found inside a brown envelope from HQ together with a metro map, a ticket, a newspaper clipping and two photographs.

Where is Mistral's rendezvous?

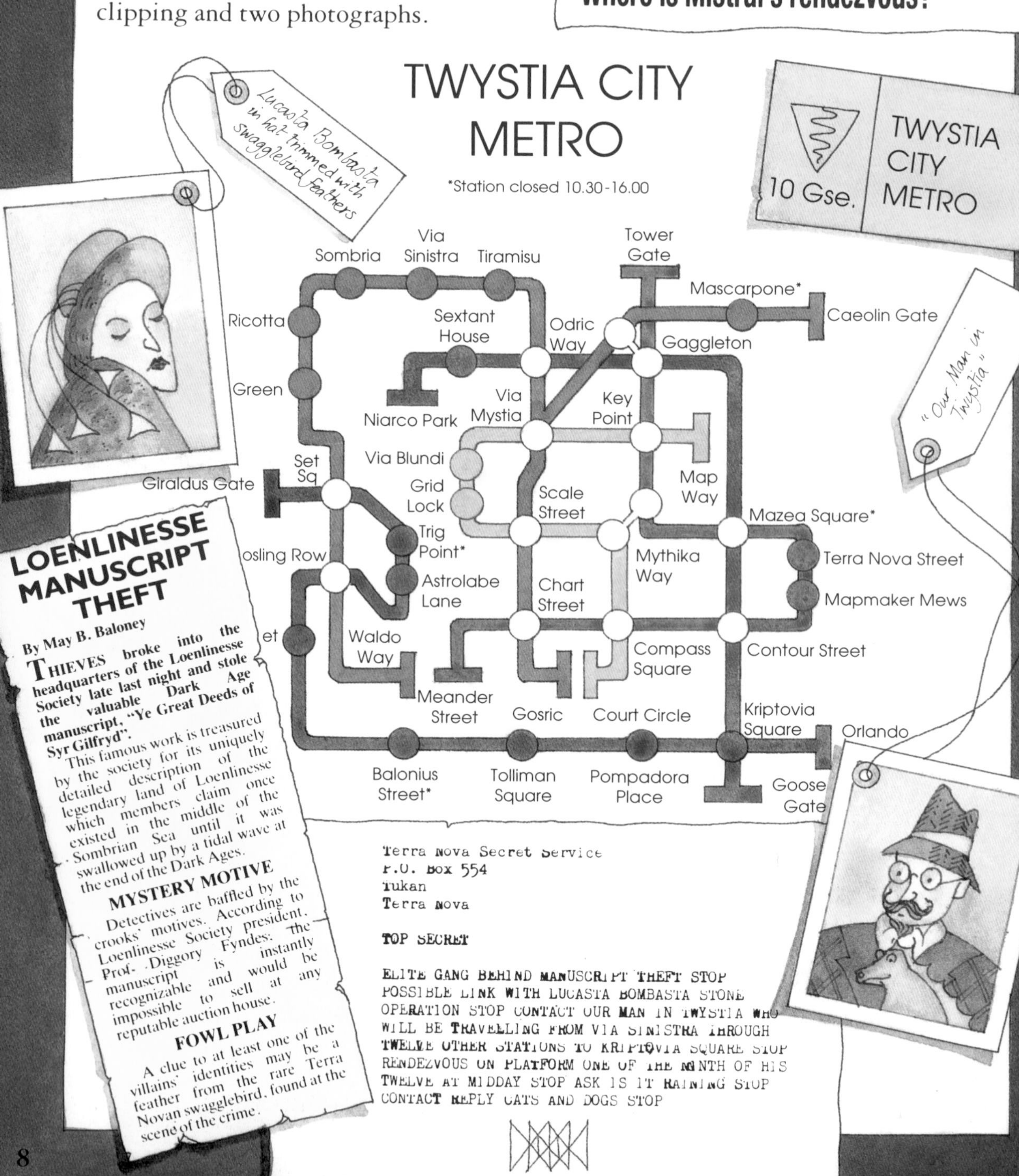

LOENLINESSE MANUSCRIPT THEFT

By May B. Baloney

THIEVES broke into the headquarters of the Loenlinesse Society late last night and stole the valuable Dark Age manuscript, "Ye Great Deeds of Syr Gilfryd".

This famous work is treasured by the society for its uniquely detailed description of the legendary land of Loenlinesse which members claim once existed in the middle of the Sombrian Sea until it was swallowed up by a tidal wave at the end of the Dark Ages.

MYSTERY MOTIVE

Detectives are baffled by the crooks' motives. According to Loenlinesse Society president, Prof. Diggory Fyndes: "The manuscript is instantly recognizable and would be impossible to sell at any reputable auction house."

FOWL PLAY

A clue to at least one of the villains' identities may be a feather from the rare Terra Novan swagglebird, found at the scene of the crime.

Terra Nova Secret Service
P.O. Box 554
Tukan
Terra Nova

TOP SECRET

ELITE GANG BEHIND MANUSCRIPT THEFT STOP
POSSIBLE LINK WITH LUCASTA BOMBASTA STONE
OPERATION STOP CONTACT OUR MAN IN TWYSTIA WHO
WILL BE TRAVELLING FROM VIA SINISTRA THROUGH
TWELVE OTHER STATIONS TO KRIPTOVIA SQUARE STOP
RENDEZVOUS ON PLATFORM ONE OF THE NINTH OF HIS
TWELVE AT MIDDAY STOP ASK IS IT RAINING STOP
CONTACT REPLY CATS AND DOGS STOP

The Deadly Dance

For her second feat, Hercula must retrieve the bouzouki of the god Karioki from the Dolmadean Dogbeasts by performing their Deadly Dance with her partner, Thrumos. This Harmonikan fresco shows the dancefloor, a great eight-pointed star, with the dancers in their starting positions. There is a total of seven moves in the dance. When it ends, all the dancers must have switched positions with the person diagonally opposite them. In a single move, each dancer twirls along the white marble way that leads straight to the next point and may go on to other points, as long as no other dancers lurk there. Hercula has to make the first move – one wrong step and the Dogbeasts will rip their rivals limb from limb.

What are the seven moves of the dance?

Orlando Bombasto's Map

In Tukan, Terra Nova's capital city, no one has heard of El Taco or the Nachos Region. The people of Tukan offer to guide Waldo Widget to the map-making town of Triangula, deep in the Terra Novan jungle. But first Waldo must find the city's lost magic charm, the Turquoise Amulet of Twitta. During his search, Waldo stumbles upon a Twystian plan of the Great Square of Tukan, together with a locket and a coded message addressed to Orlando Bombasto, a shady fellow adventurer staying in the city.

Where is the amulet?

A Hiking Map

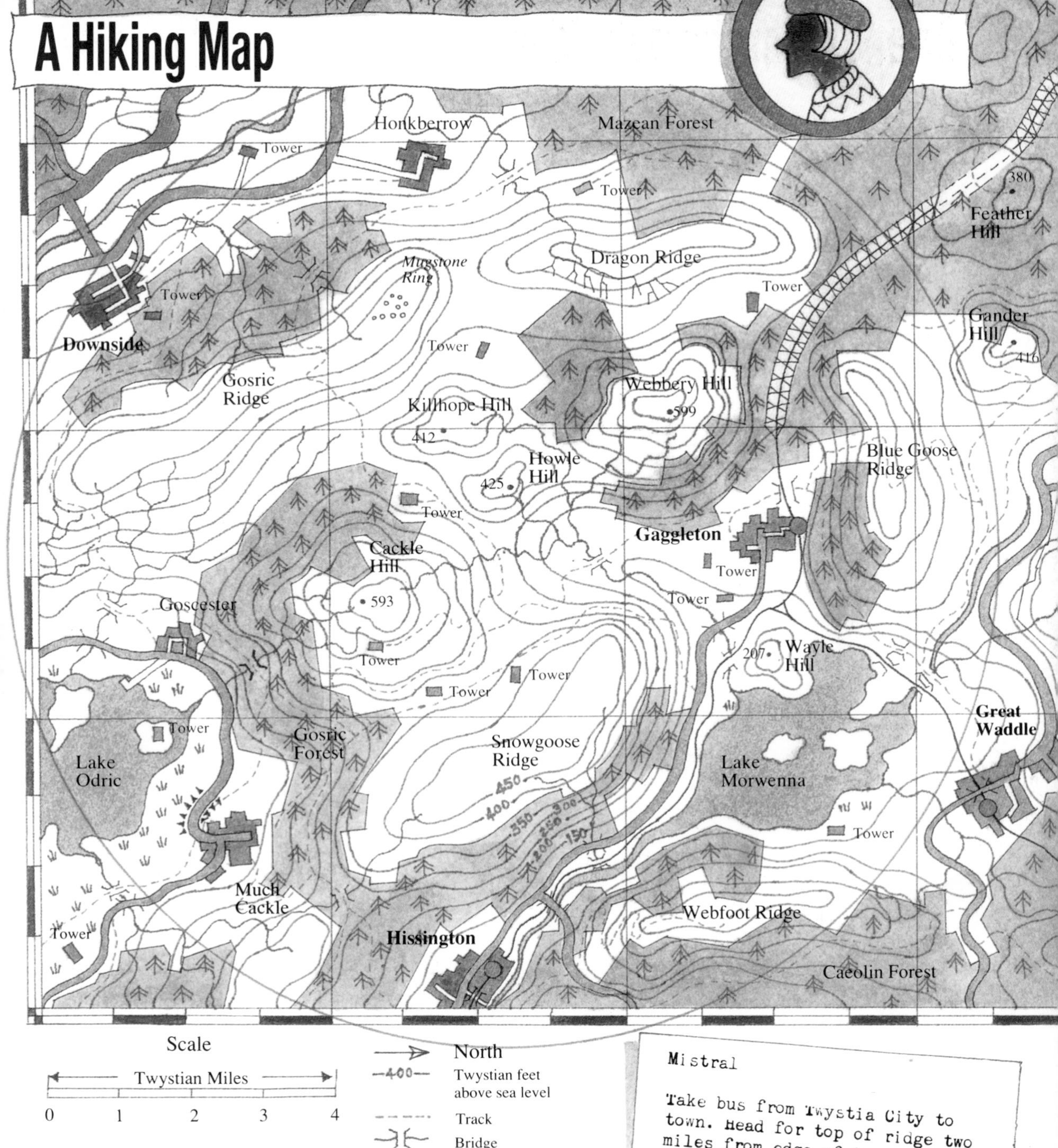

Agent Mistral's contact hands her a hiking map and directions from an informer within the Elite Gang, codenamed Cyclone. Cyclone has left a package of vital information in a ruined tower in the Twystian countryside. Mistral must collect it without delay.

What is Mistral's route?

Mistral

Take bus from Twystia City to town. Head for top of ridge two miles from edge of town. Walk along ridge to source of stream at other end. From there go four miles south-west then turn north-west and continue cross-country until you reach track. Follow track to bridge. Tower lies halfway between bridge and top of highest hill. Package is in chest by doorway.

Cyclone
NB Directions apply to area ringed in red.

The Pyramid Maze

For her third feat Hercula must retrieve the Crocodile Crown of Crocodopola, the goddess of Crocodopolis. This fabulous crown was stolen by Papyrut the magpie god and hidden in one of the chambers of the Pyramid of Ar. To find the crown, Hercula must follow a secret trail of symbols through the pyramid, guided by the cryptic contents of the scrolls of Ar. A translation of the scrolls appears on this unusual Harmonikan fresco, together with a cut-away view of the pyramid, drawn in the quirky style of Ancient Crocodopolis.

SCROLL OF AR

A TRAIL OF THREE SYMBOLS LEADS TO THE CROCODILE CROWN. ONE OR MORE OF THESE SYMBOLS APPEAR IN EACH ROOM TOGETHER WITH FALSE SYMBOLS. ENTER THE PYRAMID AND LOOK FOR THE 1ST SYMBOL IN THE 1ST ROOM, THE 2ND IN THE 2ND, THE 3RD IN THE 3RD, THEN THE 1ST IN THE 4TH, THE 2ND IN THE 5TH AND THE 3RD IN THE 6TH. CONTINUE TO FOLLOW THE TRAIL UNTIL YOU FIND THE 3RD IN THE 36TH. IN THIS ROOM YOU WILL FIND THE CROWN. BUT BEWARE - THE CURSE OF AR SHALL FALL ON ANY WHO ENTER THE SAME ROOM TWICE

Where is the Crocodile Crown?

A Plan of Fortress Howles

On the way to Lollo Rosso, a sinister stranger, the Long Knight of Howles, invites Sir Gelfrid and Hildegarde to supper at his fortress. As soon as the duo enter the castle, their host locks them in a tiny turret cell to feed to Brimstone, his greedy pet dragon for breakfast the next day. Before they can despair, a swagglebird taps on the window. It brings a plan and a picture of the fortress, together with a skeleton key, from the great enchanter, Vaeralyn.

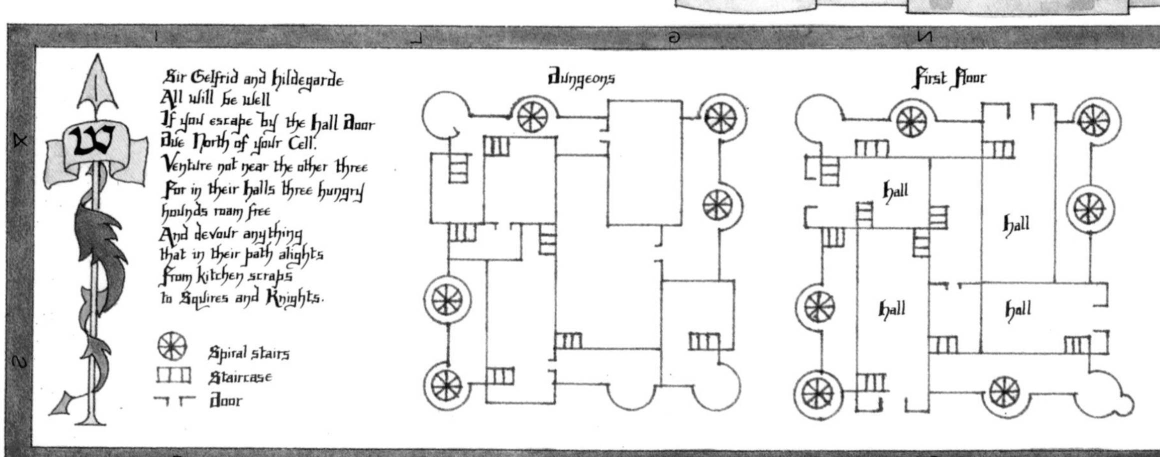

With the aid of these gifts, Gelfrid and Hildegarde plan their escape. On their way, they must rescue three other prisoners, the Knights of the Blue Goose, from the Long Knight's deepest, darkest dungeon. But they must also avoid the savage Dolmadean hounds who keep watch in three of the fortress's four great halls while the Long Knight and Brimstone sleep.

What is their route?

The Triangulan Chart

Accompanied by Orlando Bombasto and a Tukan guide, Waldo Widget reaches the town of Triangula. But the people have never heard of El Taco and seem puzzled by Balonius's map. After much debate, Waldo decides to find the Turtels who told Balonius about El Taco. The Triangulans give Waldo this map of the Terra Novan jungle to guide him, but he must turn to Balonius's diary to decipher their directions before he can work out his route.

What is Waldo's route to the Turtels?

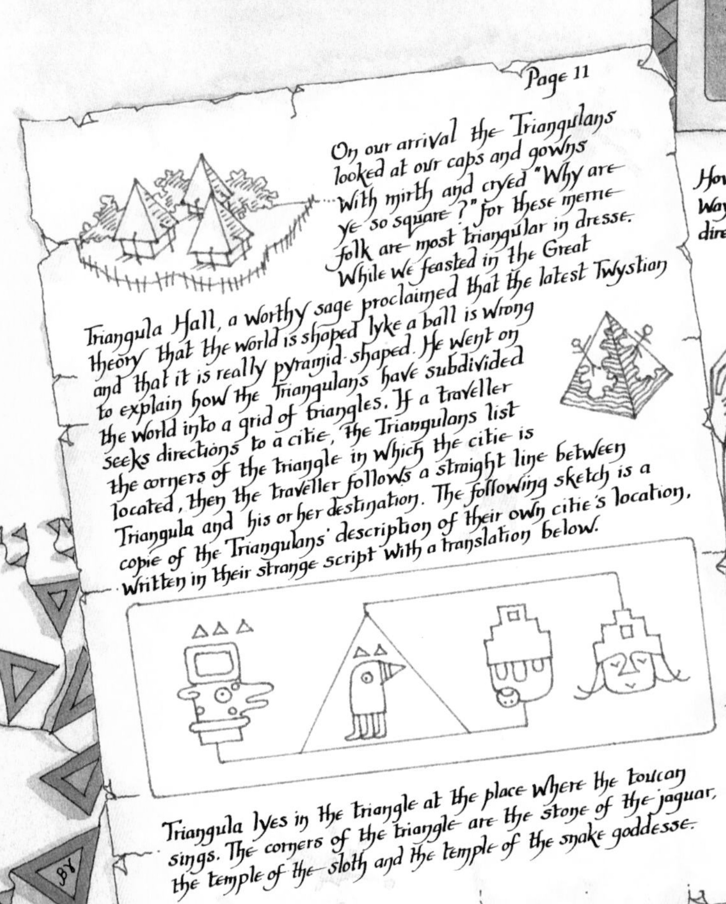

Page 11

On our arrival the Triangulans looked at our caps and gowns with mirth and cryed "Why are ye so square?" for these merrie folk are most triangular in dresse. While we feasted in the Great Triangula Hall, a worthy sage proclaimed that the latest Twystian theory that the world is shaped lyke a ball is wrong and that it is really pyramid-shaped. He went on to explain how the Triangulans have subdivided the world into a grid of triangles. If a traveller seeks directions to a citie, the Triangulans list the corners of the triangle in which the citie is located, then the traveller follows a straight line between Triangula and his or her destination. The following sketch is a copie of the Triangulans' description of their own citie's location, written in their strange script with a translation below.

Triangula lyes in the triangle at the place where the toucan sings. The corners of the triangle are the stone of the jaguar, the temple of the sloth and the temple of the snake goddesse.

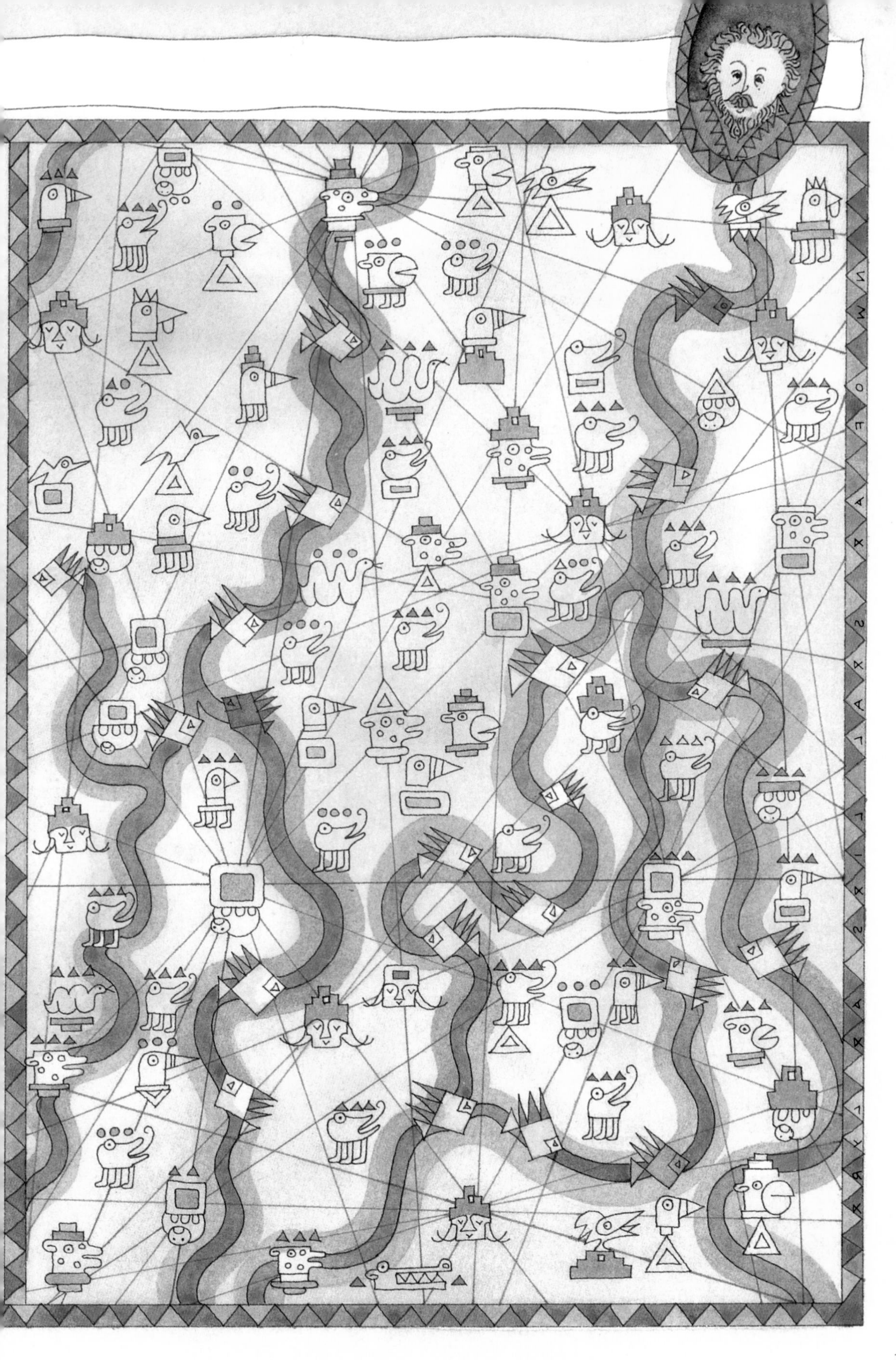

The Two Maps of Zarka City

Now Zoonal Duo has found the Crystal of Leyheyhey, his next task is to cross the Time Warp and bring it to the Planet Quirk. This may prove to be the most dangerous and difficult part of his mission, for in the entire history of space exploration, only one spaceship, under the command of Gidius of the Planet Giddio, has ever made a successful landing on the doomed planet. It was reported that Gidius passed on the secret of his landing approach route to his great-grandson, Gygyddion, an agent for the Intergalactic Agency. Unfortunately Gygyddion was captured by the Zarkans during an undercover operation in Zarka City and he is now a prisoner in the Labyrinka Prison. Accompanied by Teri Firma, an explorer from Quirk now working for the Agency, Zoonal must rescue Gygyddion, using two maps of Zarka City and the contents of an Intergalactic Intelligence File.

INTERGALACTIC INTELLIGENCE FILE

Name – GYGYDDION
Agent Number – 002
Planet of birth – GIDDIO
Mission – to enter Zarka City and search for details of secret Zarkan masterplan.
Outcome – Vital documents seized and despatched to HQ. 002 captured by Zarkan agents and taken to Labyrinka Prison.
Observations – Prison unguarded in belief that would-be rescuers will lose way in Zarka City's notorious one-way system.
Maps show: 1/ main roads
2/ enlargement of grid square (E3) where prison is located with minor roads added. X marks prison.
Intergalactic Skeleton Key will unlock all doors.

What is Zoonal's route to the prison?

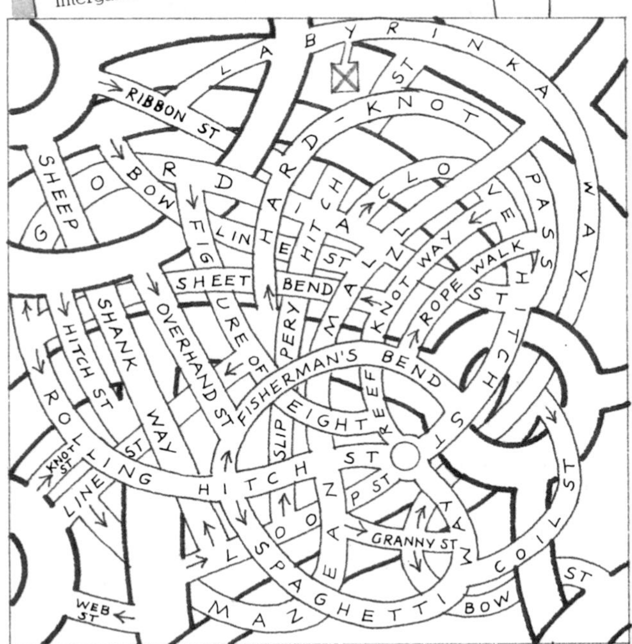

THE DECLARATION OF THE MAZE-MAKERS OF ZARKA

In the beginning, our ancestors on Quirk learned how to devise mazes. These proved to be so simple that even the most foolish of the Quirkans would eventually find the secret route.

Under our stewardship, the maze is about to reach its true destiny. By building the giant labyrinth of spaceways, Zarkan power will extend into every corner of the Ninth Universe. No one but the Zarkans will know the way between each planet, star, comet and galaxy. All who oppose us shall be sent to wander the endless loops of the giant labyrinth for eternity.

First we must remove the Planet Quirk from the path of the first spaceway. On the Quirkan day 01012100, the Great D Ray shall strike the planet at grid reference 768557. With Quirk's destruction, we shall herald the dawn of the New Era of the Planet Zarka.

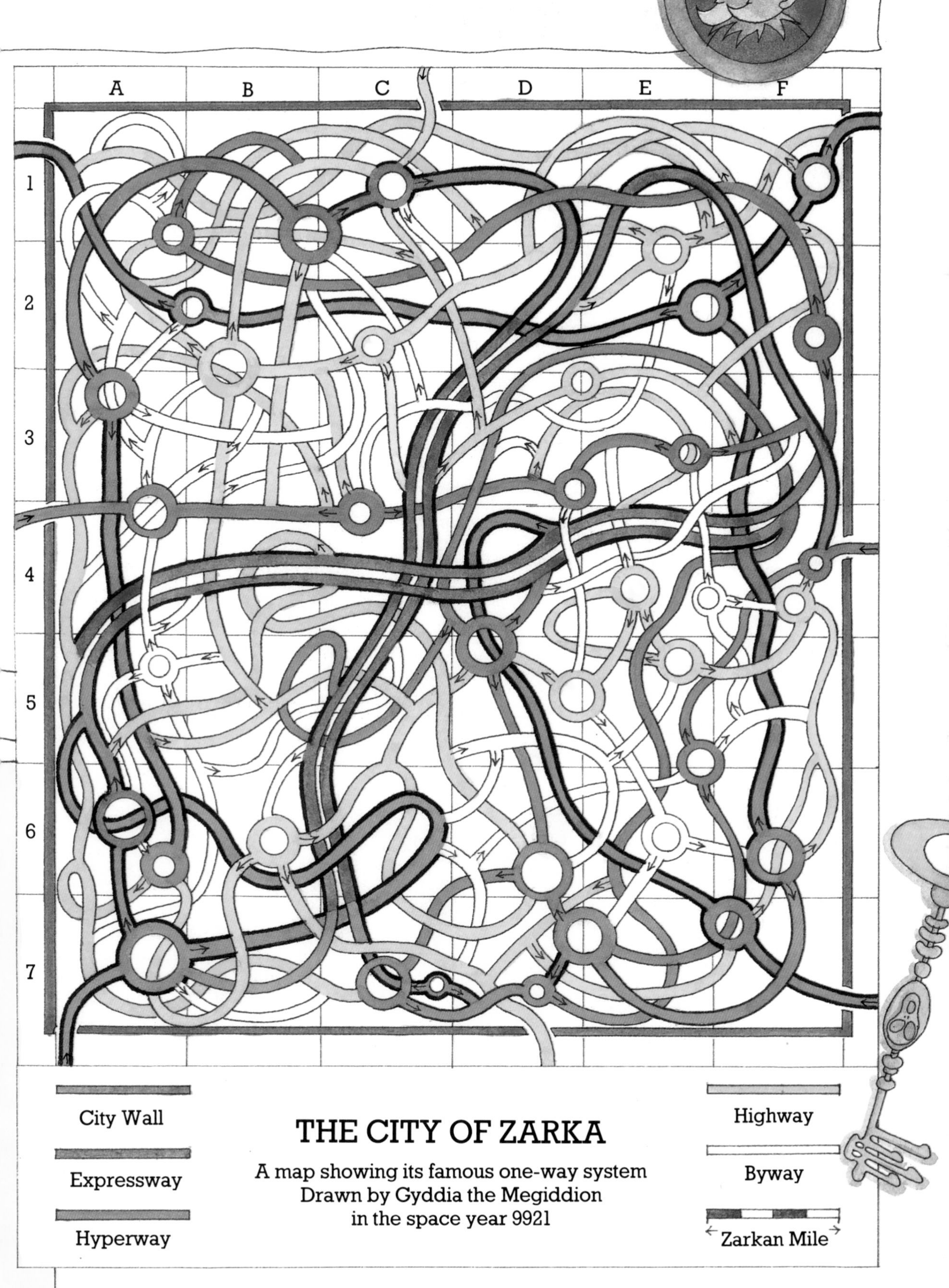
A
B
C
D
E
F
1
2
3
4
5
6
7
City Wall
Expressway
Hyperway
Highway
Byway
Zarkan Mile
THE CITY OF ZARKA
A map showing its famous one-way system
Drawn by Gyddia the Megiddion
in the space year 9921

A Plan of the Casa Fantasa

Acting on the contents of Cyclone's package, Agent Mistral prepares to enter the Casa Fantasa, the ritzy seaside retreat of the Elite Gang's leader, Lucasta Bombasta, in the land of Mascarpone. Mistral has only five minutes to find a mysterious parcel, believed to contain the stolen Mappa Blundi, and leave before the house's alarm system is activated.

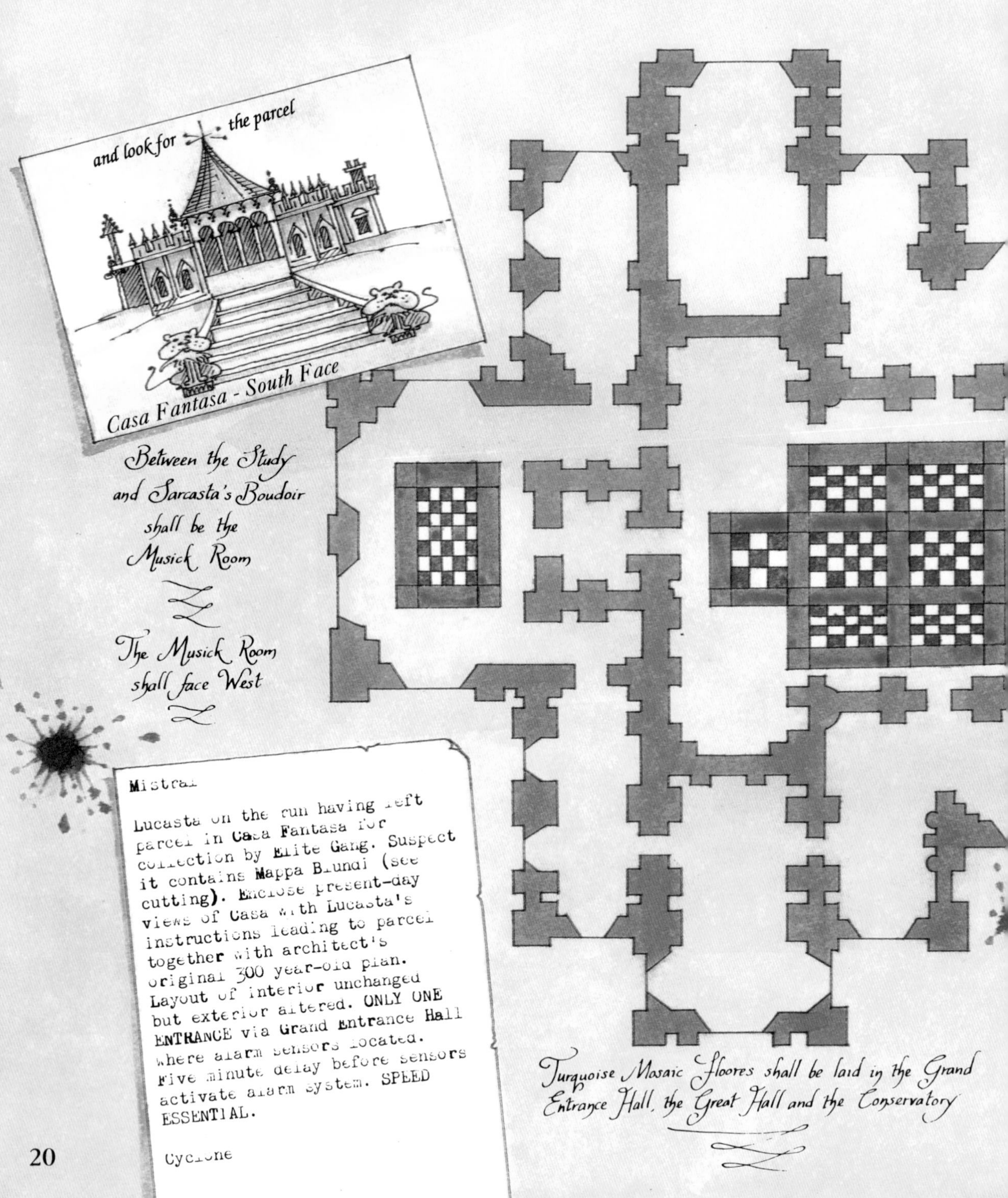

Mistral

Lucasta on the run having left parcel in Casa Fantasa for collection by Elite Gang. Suspect it contains Mappa Blundi (see cutting). Enclose present-day views of Casa with Lucasta's instructions leading to parcel together with architect's original 300 year-old plan. Layout of interior unchanged but exterior altered. ONLY ONE ENTRANCE via Grand Entrance Hall where alarm sensors located. Five minute delay before sensors activate alarm system. SPEED ESSENTIAL.

Cyclone

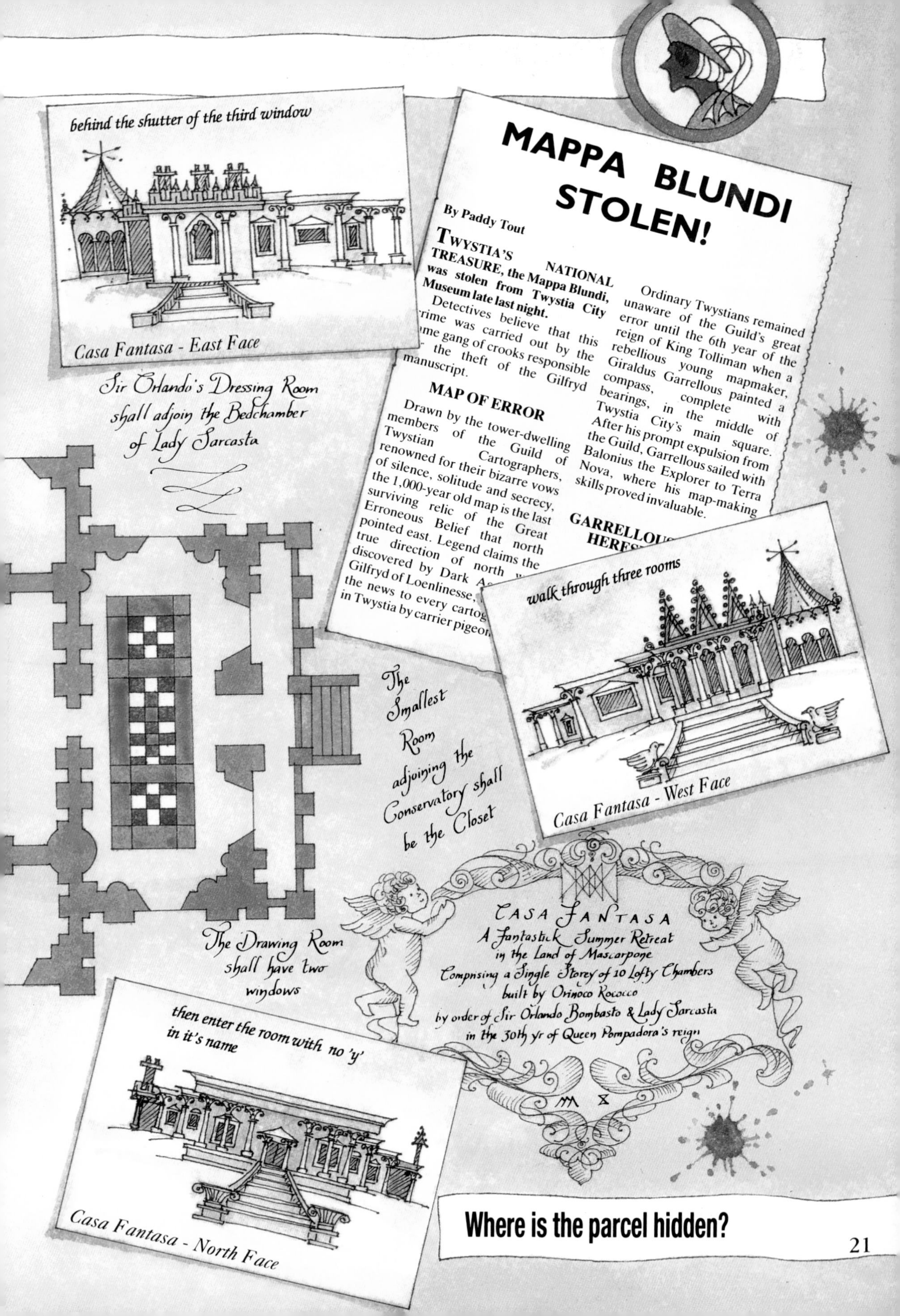

MAPPA BLUNDI STOLEN!

By Paddy Tout

TWYSTIA'S NATIONAL TREASURE, the Mappa Blundi, was stolen from Twystia City Museum late last night.

Detectives believe that this rime was carried out by the me gang of crooks responsible - the theft of the Gilfryd manuscript.

MAP OF ERROR

Drawn by the tower-dwelling members of the Twystian Guild of Cartographers, renowned for their bizarre vows of silence, solitude and secrecy, the 1,000-year old map is the last surviving relic of the Great Erroneous Belief that north pointed east. Legend claims the true direction of north w discovered by Dark A Gilfryd of Loenlinesse, the news to every cartog in Twystia by carrier pigeon

Ordinary Twystians remained unaware of the Guild's great error until the 6th year of the reign of King Tolliman when a rebellious young mapmaker, Giraldus Garrellous painted a compass, complete with bearings, in the middle of Twystia City's main square. After his prompt expulsion from the Guild, Garrellous sailed with Balonius the Explorer to Terra Nova, where his map-making skills proved invaluable.

GARRELLOU HERES

The Labyrinth of Amphibia

For her fourth feat, Hercula must bring the Magic Blancmange of Baklava to Semolino, the youngest of the Five Princes of Twystia. The goddess Amphibia imprisoned the five princes in her labyrinth, depicted on this Harmonikan fresco, and decreed that each would turn into a frog on their 8th birthday, as a punishment for stealing her five sacred tadpoles. The spell will be broken if

Semolino eats the Magic Blancmange before his 8th birthday. Unfortunately Hercula has only five minutes to find her way through the labyrinth and reach him before it is too late.

What is Hercula's route?

A Map of Lollo Rosso

At last Sir Gelfrid and Hildegarde reach the kingdom of Lollo Rosso with 20 Twystian geese and a bag of gold, a reward from the three Knights of the Blue Goose. They are disguised as goose traders, for Bombastus the evil ruler of Lollo Rosso has decreed that only geese and their owners are allowed into his realm. Using this goose trader's map, Gelfrid and Hildegarde must decide which of Lollo Rosso's four gates to enter before they make their way through a maze of towns and tollgates to Bombastus's Castle where the Singing Rock lies hidden.

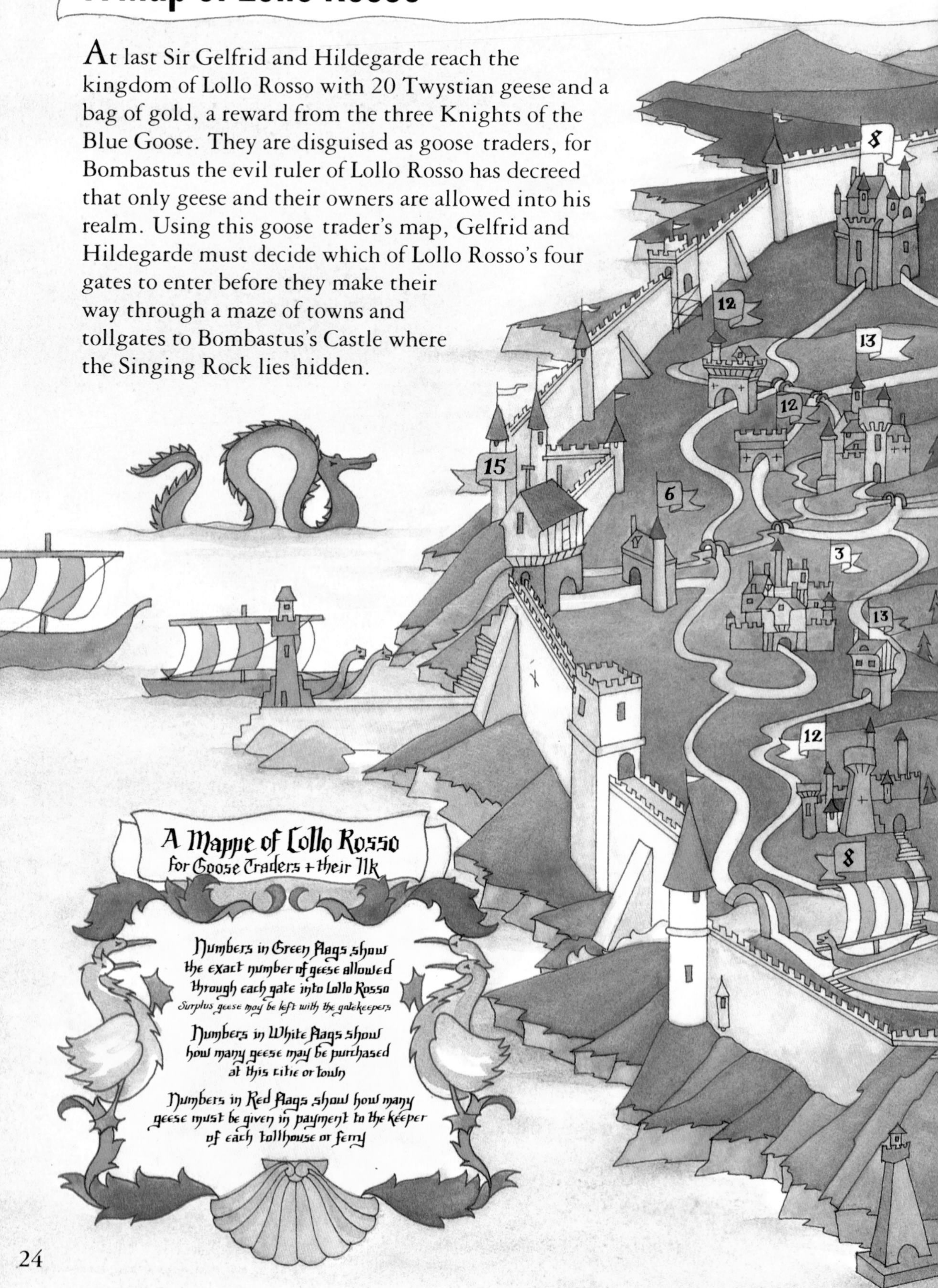

What is their route?

A Map of Bokonsrikta

Friday
Ditermined to have Golden Idle for fowntain at Chateau Niarco, I sett off for Grate Temple of Pythonia on morn of Bokonsrikta's 15th Pythonic Games. As customerrie during Games, citie desserted except for 3 gards keeping watch frum 3 towers. Guards had good view down streetes radiating frum areas around their towers, but that was all they coulde see, for their towers are not veri tall. I kept to backstreetes and courtyardes, except for 11 occasions when I hadde to rush across streetes within view of towers. Luckilie I coulde see when guards turned their heads before I made my moove. At last I reached a dustie courtyard surrounded by houses on 3½ sides. In middle stude Grate Temple of Pythonia - a huge stepped pyramidd with 2 redde stones on its summit. I

On his way to the Turtel people, Waldo Widget is captured by snake charmers from Bokonsrikta. They take Waldo back to their city and lock him in the Temple of Pythonia, the snake goddess, to juggle with ten venomous snakes in the 20th Pythonic Games the next day. Waldo turns to Balonius's diary, only to discover that his bag has been switched. The bag in its place contains a length of bright material, a locket, a letter, a page from a diary, a Twystian map of Bokonsrikta and a key. Although these items won't help Waldo with his snake juggling, they will help him escape from the city.

What is Waldo's safest escape route?

To my most worthless son Orlando

Repair your low position in my esteem by fynding the Stone of Bombastus that was yielded unto our renowned ancestor by vanquished Harmonikans at the dawn of the great Dark Age, then mysteriouslie loste. A clue to its fate may lye in this fragment of material. A picture on its border shows the Stone in the handes of two strangelie-costumed folke. As my olde friend, Marco Niarco, found the fragment in Bokonsrikta, I fancy that this Terra Novan citie may holde the secret of the Stone's hiding place. Therefore I urge you to hasten to Bokonsrikta and search every temple and dwelling with the aid of this skeleton key and mappe which Marco hath kindlie lent us, together with a page from his journal.

On your way to Bokonsrikta, forget not to collect the Turquoise Amulet of Twitta from the citie of Tukan. Before he set off for Bokonsrikta, Marco took the amulet and hid it somewhere safe. So thrilled was he with his Bokonsriktan booty that he forgot to retrieve the amulet before sailing home to Twystia.

Your loving mother

Agrippina

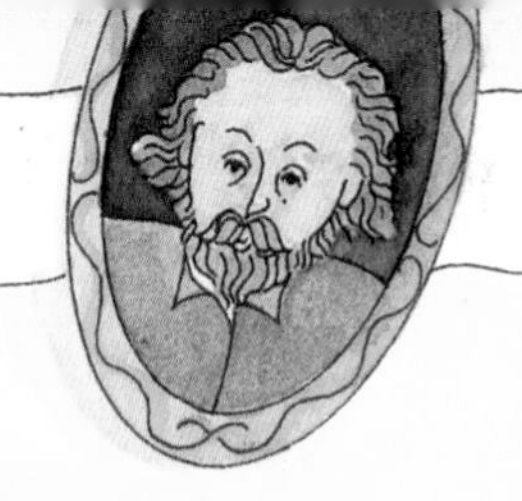

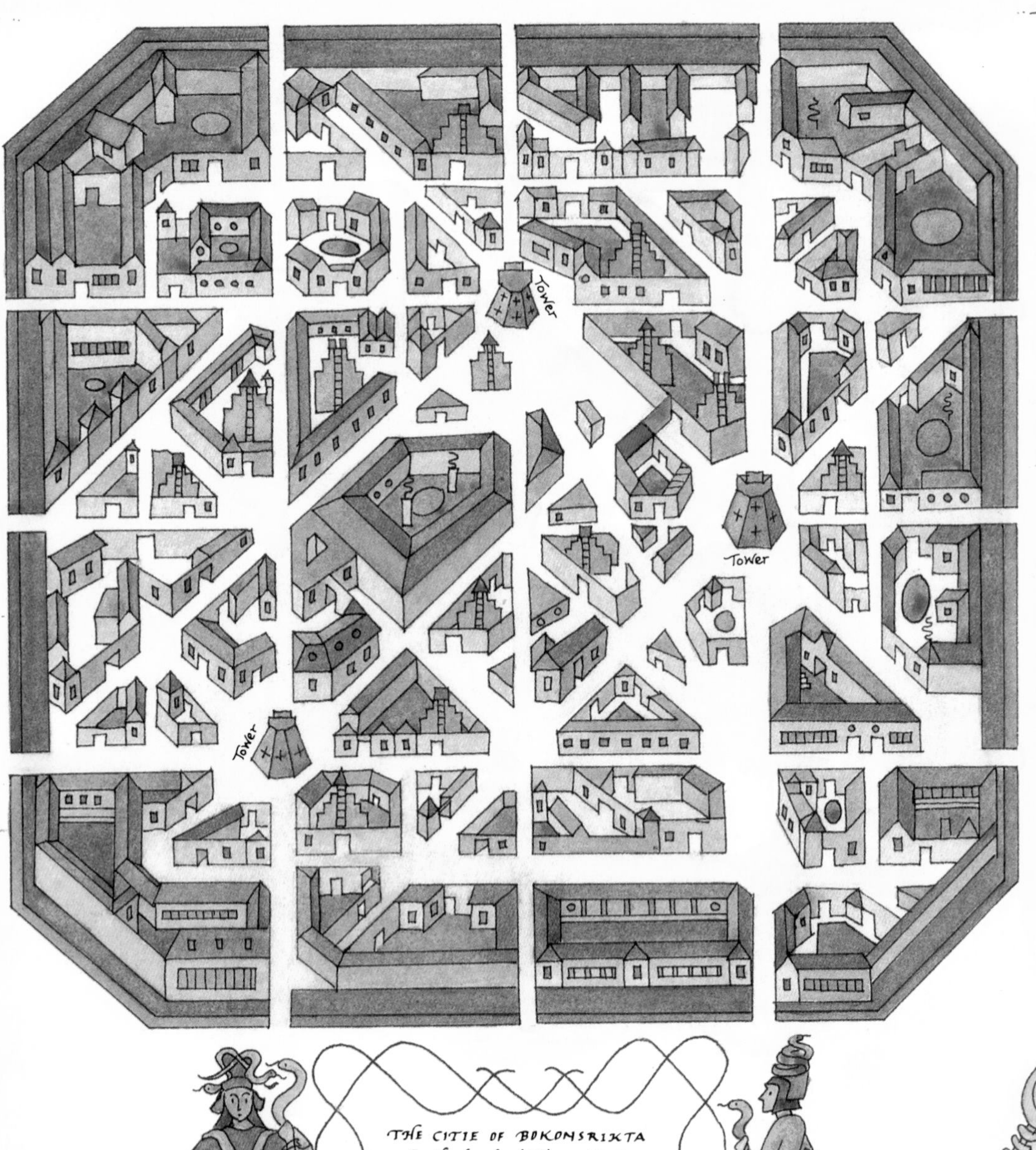

THE CITIE OF BOKONSRIKTA
In the lande of Terra Nova

Showing its streets, its temples
its dwelling houses, its three watch-
towers & its 12 city gates

Drawne for Marco Hiarco
Esq.

By the Guild of Twystian Cartographers
in the fifth yeare of the reign of Queen
Pompadora

The Treasure Chart of Gidius

from the gytower on the gshores of Gmegiddio walk ΣM to the griver and follow it to its gsource. from there turn GM and travel 50 glygs in that gydirection before heading due M. When you are due G of the temple gydoor, make your gyway ΣM to the gybank of the second griver then go 75 glygs M and 50 glygs G. This will bring you to the gspot in the gypastures by the gmountains where my gychest lies buried.

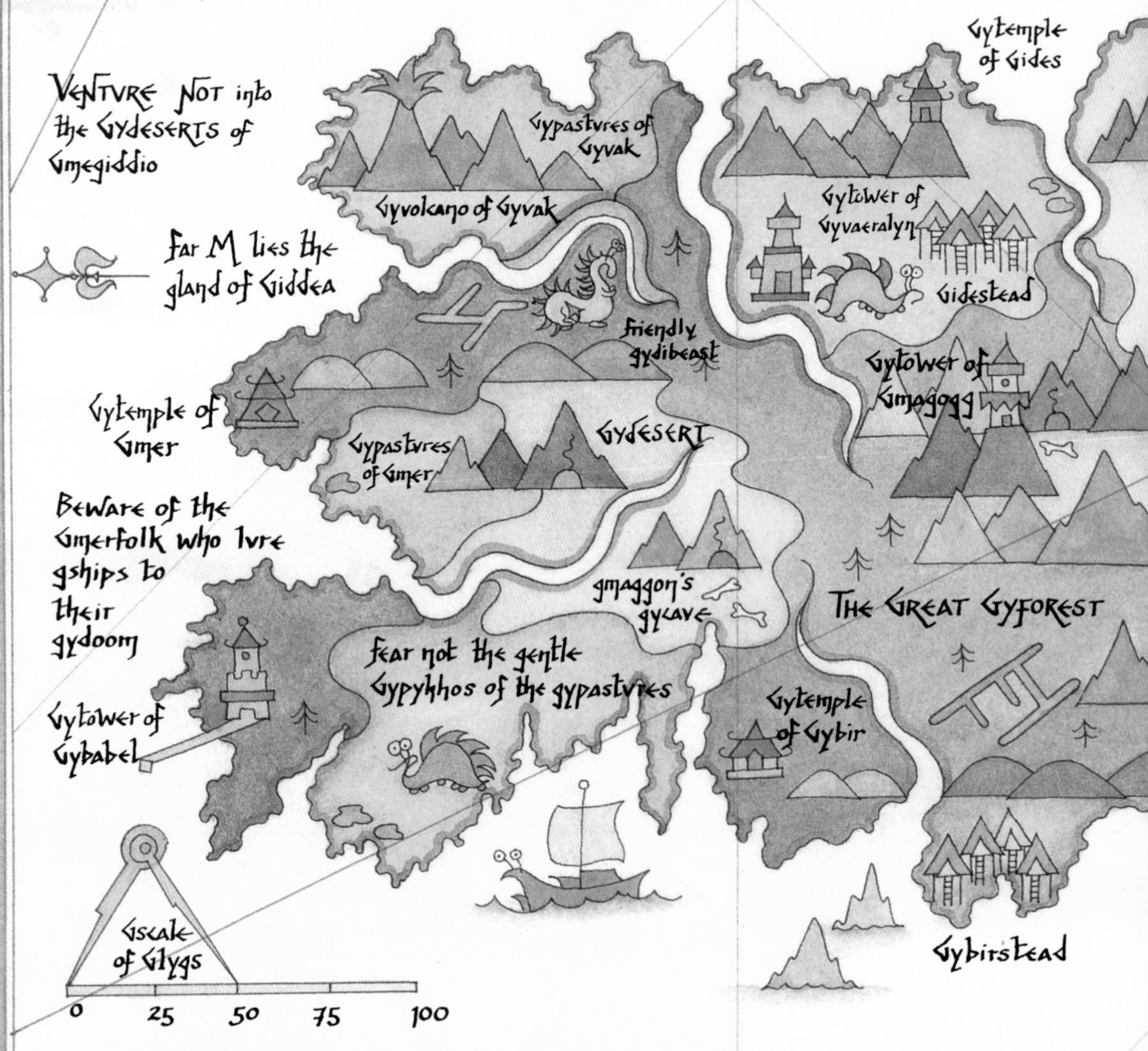

After Zoonal Duo and Teri Firma release Gygyddion from his Zarkan prison, he joins the mission to bring the Crystal of Leyheyhey to the Planet Quirk. But Gygyddion does not know the safe route to the surface of the doomed planet. The vital information was buried in a chest on the island of Megiddio on the Planet Giddio by his ancestor, Gidius, who led the only successful expedition to Quirk.

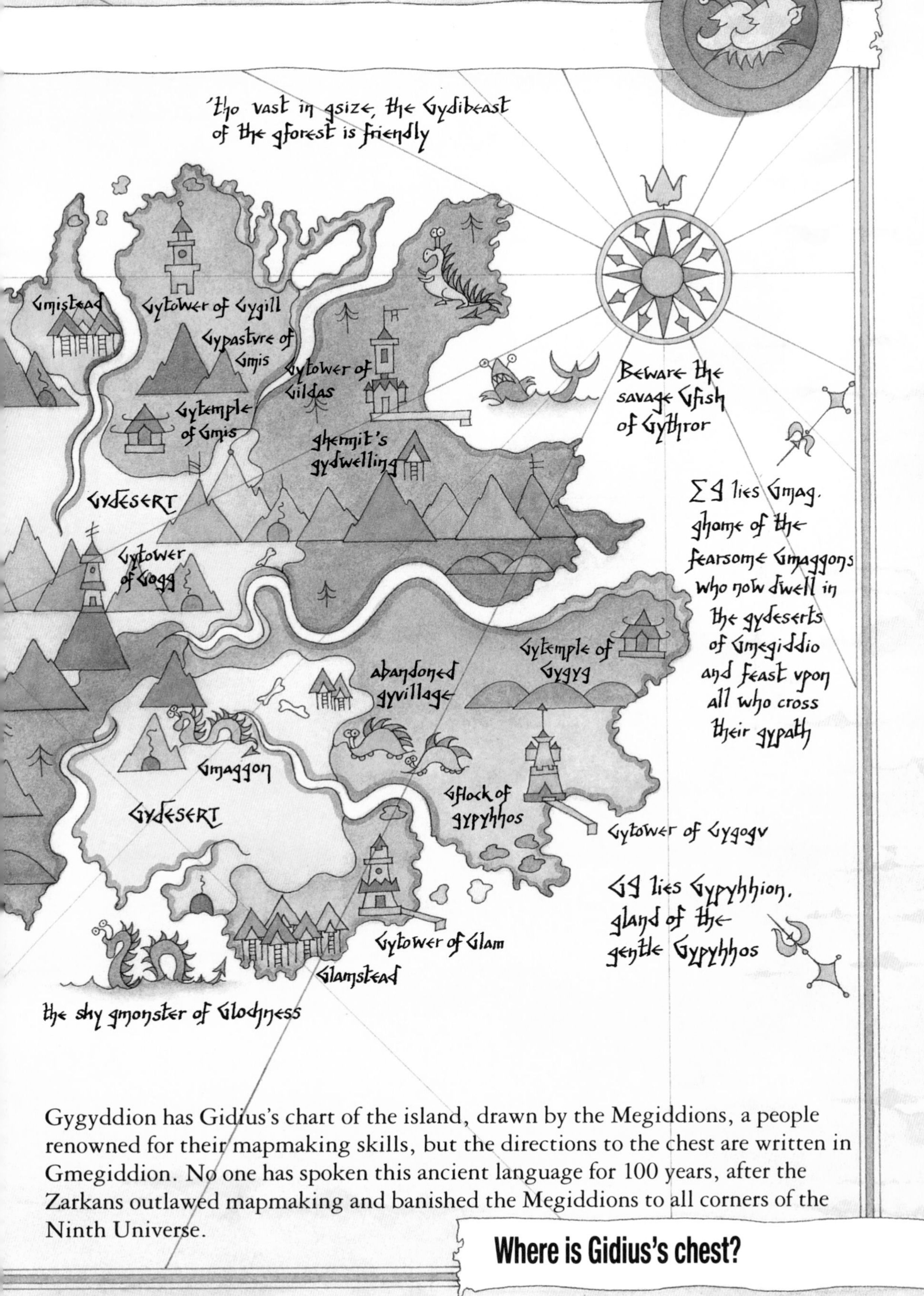

Gygyddion has Gidius's chart of the island, drawn by the Megiddions, a people renowned for their mapmaking skills, but the directions to the chest are written in Gmegiddion. No one has spoken this ancient language for 100 years, after the Zarkans outlawed mapmaking and banished the Megiddions to all corners of the Ninth Universe.

Where is Gidius's chest?

The Flight Chart

Inside the Casa Fantasa, Agent Mistral finds a parcel containing a letter from the Elite Gang's elusive leader, Lucasta Bombasta, and six envelopes addressed to her six fellow gang members. Inside each envelope is a set of six airline tickets leading to Lucasta's secret location. As a result of her complex itinerary, cunningly designed to throw detectives off her trail, the gangsters' journey will take three days. With the aid of a flight chart, can Agent Mistral find a swifter route to the crooks' mystery destination?

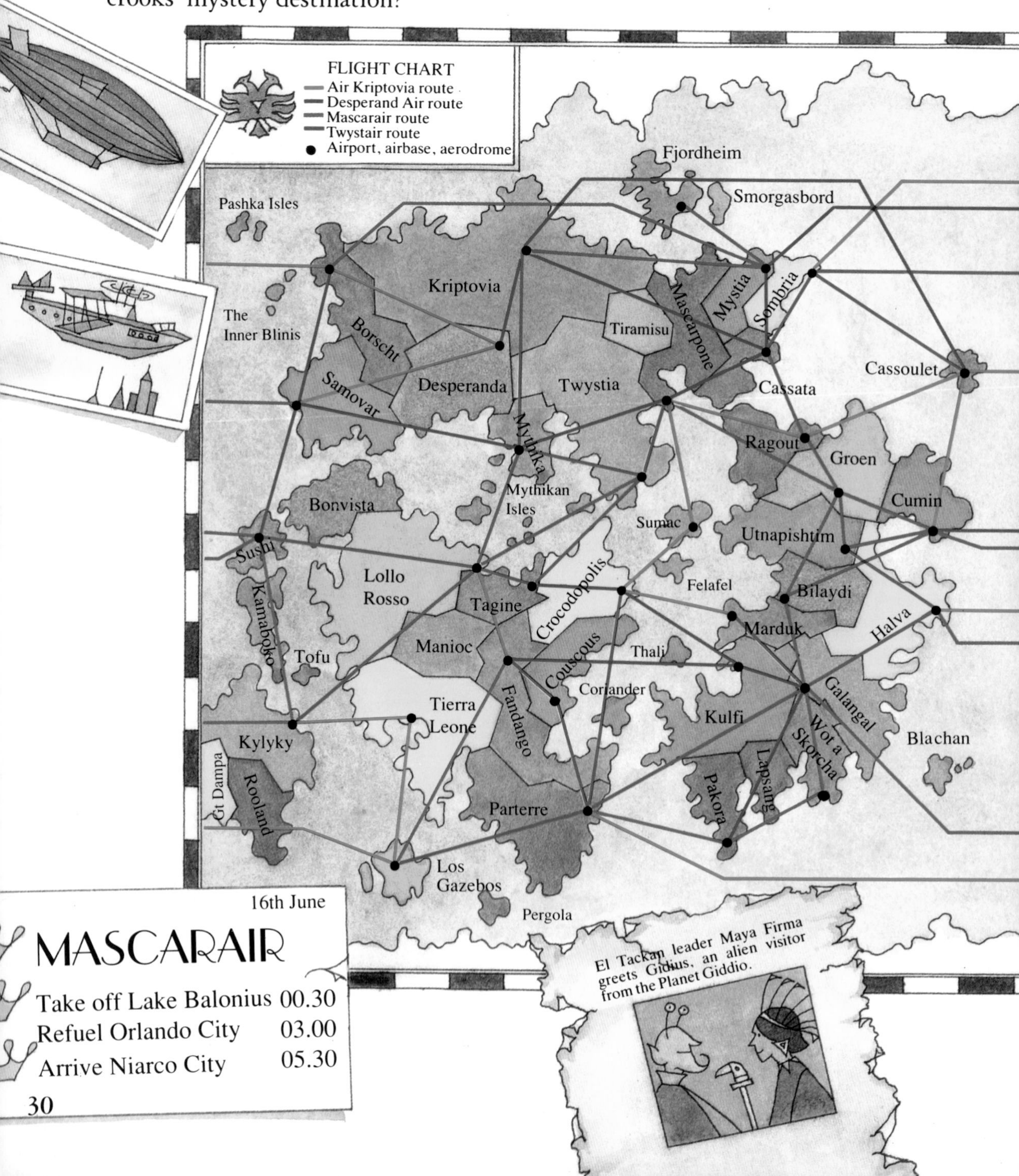

Desperand Air

16th/17th June

Take off Hercula Falls	21.15
Refuel Brimstone Basin	00.15
Arrive Rococco Airbase	01.15

TWYSTAIR

15th June

Take off Ricotta	17.30
Refuel Gosric	18.50
Refuel Gelfriston	21.45
Arrive Lake Balonius	23.50

14th June

Apologies for my sudden disappearance. The Twystian police are on my trail after they found a swagglebird feather from my hat in the Loenlinesse Society's HQ. Luckily our mission is almost at an end and soon the Stone of Bombastus will be in my hands. I have left sets of six air tickets for each of you. With these you must board the airship at Ricotta Aerodrome in Mascarpone disguised as Mythikan folk-dancers and lead detectives on a wild goose chase across the globe. When you reach your final destination, head for the harbour due south of the airfield, where I shall be waiting aboard my launch, The Lady Agrippina.

Lucasta

16th June

Air Kriptobia

Take off Niarco City	10.30
Refuel Thrumos City	12.30
Refuel Blondi Airbase	14.40
Arrive Hudlum City	16.50

TWYSTAIR

17th June

Take off Rococco Airbase	04.45
Arrive Port Vaeralyn	06.00

MASCARAIR

16th June

Take off Hudlum City
Arrive Hercula Falls

What is Mistral's most direct route?

The Harmonikan Map

For her fifth and final feat, Hercula must find the Jewel of Joy. Long ago, Tikitaka, a sailor from a distant land presented this magical jewel to the gloomy Hypokondryad, the most beautiful of the immortals, after she announced that she would marry the mortal who could make her smile. Little did Tikitaka know that the Hypokondryad enjoyed being miserable so the Jewel of Joy just made sure that no one would ever succeed in making her smile.

Other suitors came, but their quest was doomed. Eventually they gave up and soon everyone forgot where the Hypokondryad lived or whether she existed. With the aid of the Mythikan Deities' map of the world, depicted on this Harmonikan fresco, can Hercula track down the Hypokondryad and the Jewel of Joy and win the Golden Ladle of Heroism?

Where is the Hypokondryad?

The Path Perilous

Still in disguise, Sir Gelfrid and Hildegarde step inside the Enchanted Hall of Bombastus's Castle. Across a checkered floor, diagonally opposite them, stands the Singing Rock, bathed in a mysterious blue light. Now they must find the invisible Path Perilous that leads to the magical rock and the end of their quest. But they must beware, for if they stray from the path, they will turn into wax figures. Their only guide is this strange painting of the castle from Vaeralyn the Enchanter. In the middle is the checkered floor, with the duo and the rock in their respective positions. Unlike the real floor, this painted floor is bordered with triangles, each bearing a number. Could these numbers, together with the small checkerboard on the right of the painting, hold the key to finding the Path Perilous?

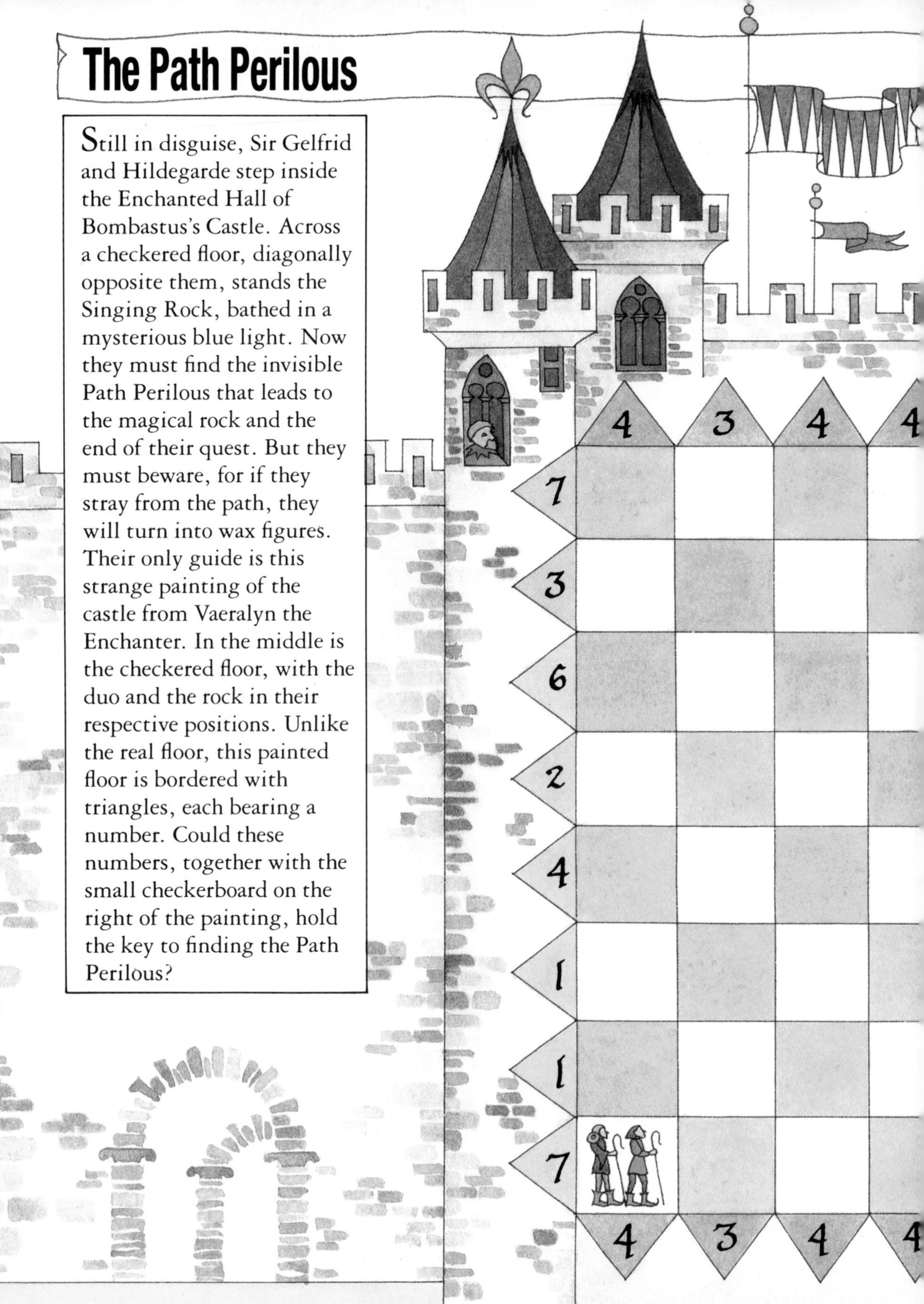

5 3 7 1
7
3
6
2
4
1
1
7
5 3 7 1
4 3 2 2
4 4
3 3
2 2
2 2
4 3 2 2
The Snake on this chequered board of aspect bizarre
Follows a route not seen by eye, the fabled Way of Ar.
Identical in principle yet harder in the test
Is that invisible Path Perilous you must tread to end your quest.
The numbers in the gold triangles display
How many squares in each row form part of the Way
While the numbers in the blue triangles show
Through how many squares in each column
the Way doth go.
Upwards, downwards and sideways the Way winds
But ne'er doth it travel in diagonal lines.
Where is the Path Perilous?

The Coded Carpet Map

After a narrow escape from Bokonsrikta, Sir Waldo Widget stumbles upon the remote jungle town of Chirpeecheep, birthplace of Twitta, the founder of Tukan. To Waldo's relief, not only have the people of Chirpeecheep heard of the Nachos Region but they actually know where the city of El Taco is. During a great feast, they supply Waldo with a set of puzzling directions, which he writes in his diary, and present him with a strange compass and a tapestry carpet. The carpet's geometric pattern is a coded map of the roads, towns, mountains, rivers and tunnels of the Nachos Region. Using the compass, Waldo must locate Chirpeecheep and El Taco on the carpet map, before he can plot his route to the legendary city.

What is Waldo's route to El Taco?

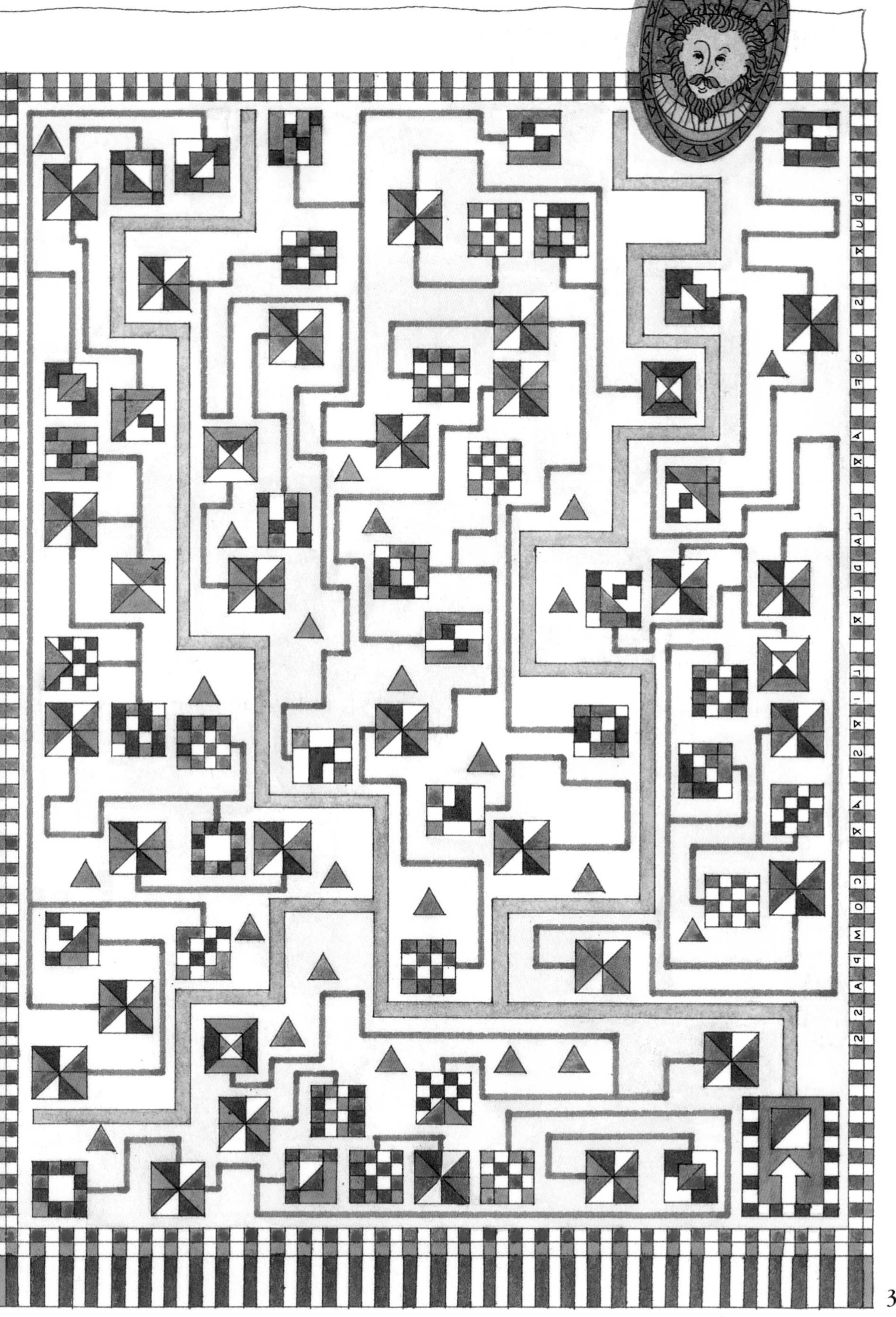

The Coded Map of Terra Nova

Zoonal Duo, Teri Firma and Gygyddion finally cross the Great Time Warp and prepare to land on the Planet Quirk. No one knows which time zone they have entered, but all three hope that they can bring the Crystal of Leyheyhey to the doomed planet before the Zarkans strike. Now Zoonal must find the landing approach route of Gidius, Gygyddion's great-grandfather and the leader of the only successful expedition to Quirk. To guide him, Zoonal has a log book written in Gmegiddion and a faded map of the Quirkan land of Terra Nova, which he found inside Gidius's chest on the Planet Giddio. Unfortunately Gidius's route is shown on the map using a cunning code.

Cartographers

0	0	0	0	0	1	0
0	0	0	0	1	2 X	1
1	1	0	1	2	3	1
3	3	2	3	3	3	1
2	3	2	3	3	1	0
2	3	2	3	3	1	0
2	3	2	2	3	1	0
2	3	3	3	3	1	0
1	2	3	3	3	1	0
0	0	1	1	1	0	0
0	0	0	0	0	0	0

ENCHILLADA

NOVA

R. Twitta

Tukan

44 46 48 50 52 54 56 58 60 62

86 88 90 92 94 96

NOVA

N

Miles

250 300

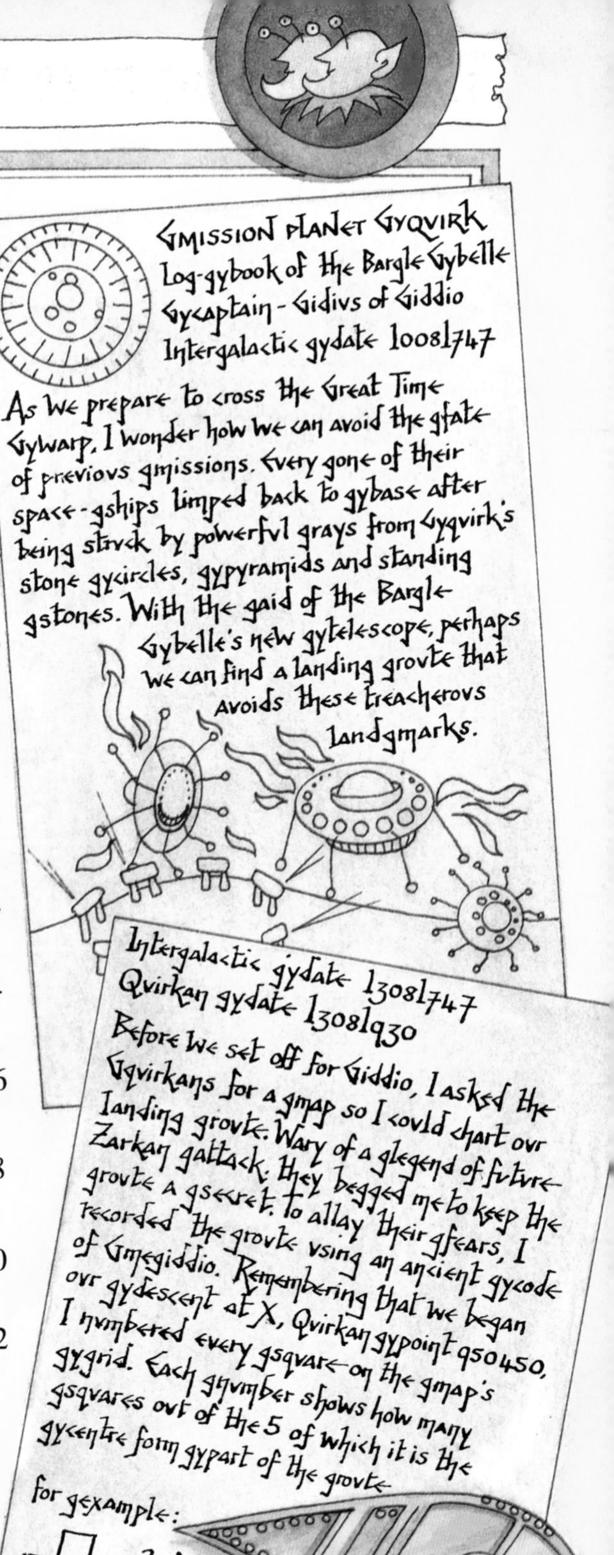

What is the safe landing route?

The Chart of Loenlinesse

After crossing the Time Warp, Zoonal Duo, Teri Firma and Gygyddion arrived on the Planet Quirk just after the dawn of civilization and brought the Crystal of Leyheyhey to the town of El Taco. Centuries later, an El Tackan sailor, Tikitaka, gave the Crystal to the Hypokondryad who lived in the distant land of Twystia. The Crystal, now known as the Jewel of Joy, was retrieved by Hercula and presented to the people of Harmonika. At the dawn of the Dark Age of the Seven Kingdoms, the Jewel, now called the Singing Rock, was stolen by

A QUESTION OF JEWEL IDENTITY

WHILE bird-watching on the island of Harmonika, Milo Midnight of Middle-Knight-on-Sea stumbled over a chocolate cake plate dating from the dawn of Mythikan civilization.

The platter depicts the mythical heroine Hercula handing the Jewel of Joy to a Harmonikan islander.

According to Prof Ouzo Spurios, the blue Jewel is none other than the Crystal of Leyheyhey, a legendary stone which appears on an ancient Terra Novan carpet, now in Tukan Museum.

CRYSTAL SPACE MISSION

ROSY PARKER, Chief Reporter

EARLY today, Teri Firma of El Taco, Terra Nova, set off across the Time Warp into the Ninth Universe. Her mission is to find the lost Crystal of Leyheyhey.

ALIEN LEGEND

Legend says the Crystal was brought to El Taco by three aliens to protect our planet from destruction by the Planet Zarka.

Teri Firma hopes to travel back in time and beat the alien trio to the Crystal. What will happen next is unclear. In the last 50 years of space exploration, no mission ha returned to Quirk.

After crossing the Enchanted Halle of Bombastus's Castle, Syr Gilfryd and Hyldagerd claimed the Singing Rocke and made haste to return to the kingdom of Loenlinesse with their prize. And lo, as they galloped across the Great Bridge of Loenlinesse bearing the magicall Rocke, trees blossomed, flowers bloomed, corn ripened, birdes sang and joy returned at last to that beleaguered lande.

Whenne they reached the Citie of Loenlinesse, Syr Gilfryd and Hyldagerd rode straight to the Great Palace and presented the Singing Rocke to Queen Ethelwalda. The gentle monarch entrusted the Rocke to her loyall counsellor, Vaeralinna the Enchanter, who took it to her tower twixt the Palace and Towne of Midmarsh and locked it in a bejewelled casket.

Sadlie, as the yeares passed, the people of Loenlinesse forgot about the Rocke, the source of their happinesse and prosperitie, and grew idle and selfish. No one repaired Loenlinesse's crumblinge dams and river bankes, or heeded the rising level of the Great Sea. And so one stormie night, Loenlinesse was submerged by a great Flood and her people were forced to seek shelter in neighbouring landes.

ELITE OUTWITTED

LATE last night, Elite Gang leader Lucasta Bombasta was arrested aboard her launch off the Sombrian coast.

Inside Lucasta's luxury launch, detectives found the stolen manuscript, "Ye Great Deeds of Syr Gilfryd" the priceless Mappa Blundi, and a mysterious Dark Age casket.

Other members of the Elite Gang were rounded up in Mascarpone. Police have denied reports that they acted on a tip-off from Terra Nova's Secret Service.

Bombastus of Lollo Rosso. According to "Ye Great Deeds of Syr Gilfryd", the Rock was rescued by Sir Gelfrid and Hildegarde who brought it to the lost land of Loenlinesse. In the Great Gang Era, a descendant of Bombastus, Lucasta Bombasta, recovered an ancient casket from the depths of the Sombrian Sea. It contained this tattered chart of an unknown land, which some believe to be Loenlinesse. Whether the chart holds the secret of the Singing Rock's fate remains a mystery, for no one has been able to decipher its strange writing.

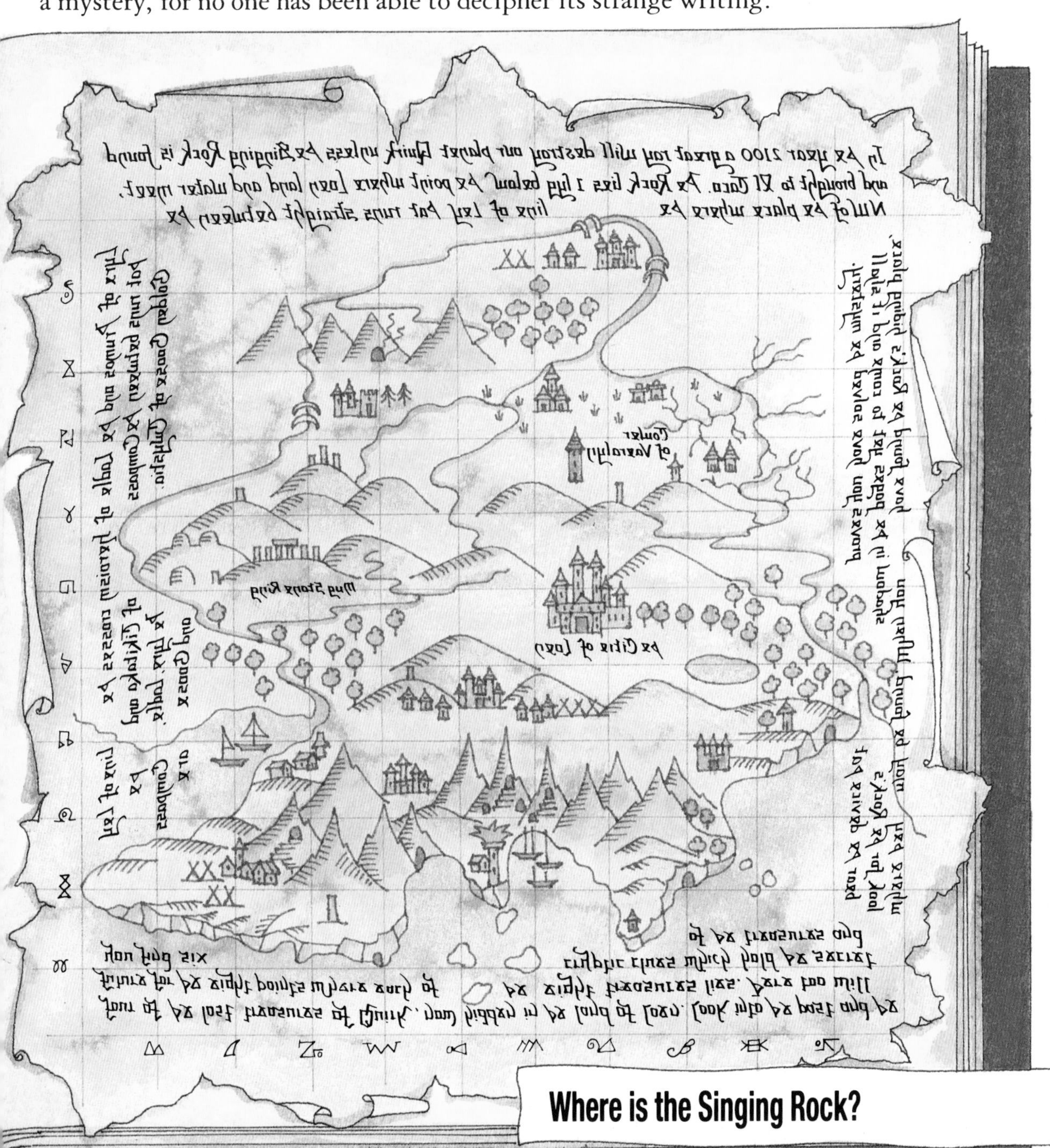

Where is the Singing Rock?

Clues

Page 4
Remember not to follow the same starway twice.

Page 5
Watch out! Some tunnels lead to dead ends.

Page 6
What does the strange inscription on the map plate say? Could Balonius's diary hold the key?

Page 7
Solve this by a process of elimination. Which cities can you rule out? The cryptic clues assume that Mappa Blundi is pointing north.

Page 8
Can you find a route between Via Sinistra and Kriptovia Square that passes through 12 other stations? What time is Mistral's rendezvous?

Page 9
There are only seven moves in the dance, so one dancer can only move once. Remember the dancers may go through several points in one move – even the point they are aiming for.

Page 10
What does the coded message say? Look at the strange design on Orlando Bombasto's locket case. Could it hold the key?

Page 11
Try following Cyclone's directions from each of the towns. Which direction is the map facing?

Pages 12-13
Read the scrolls carefully. Find the secret symbols by a process of elimination then follow them in their correct order. Beware of the curse of Ar.

Pages 14-15
Can you locate the turret cell, the knights' dungeon and the safe hall door on the plan? Where is north? This is a three-dimensional maze.

Pages 16-17
Can you find symbols on the map which match those in the diary?

Pages 18-19
Find the route to the prison on the small map first so you know which major road to aim for on the large map. Look out for the direction arrows at the start of each road.

Pages 20-21
Try combining the words above the pictures of the Casa Fantasa to form a message. Now match up the pictures with the plan. Can you locate most of the rooms using the architect's notes? How many windows does each room have in Mistral's time?

Pages 22-23
Make sure you have a pencil and an eraser.

Pages 24-25
Try each route and make a note of how many geese you gain and lose.

Pages 26-27
Read the diary carefully. Where is the Temple of Pythonia? Can you find a road leading out of the city that is not overlooked by any of the three towers?

Pages 28-29
What are the points of the Megiddion compass? Which direction is the chart pointing?

Pages 30-31
Try putting the tickets in order. Can you find the gangsters' route on the map? Which country are they starting from?

Pages 32-33
Follow the directions from each of the ports of the labyrinth. Where is north?

Pages 34-35
Solve this by a process of elimination. Remember the Path Perilous can only cross a line of squares headed by 1 once. This means that every square forming the path in the previous rows or columns must be found before Gelfrid and Hildegarde can cross these lines.

Pages 36-37
Look at the symbol in the red box at the bottom righthand corner of the map. Could it show which direction the map is pointing? The diagonal lines on the town symbols will help you find the exact locations of El Taco and Chirpeecheep.

Pages 38-39
Once you understand the principle of Gidius's code, the rest is easy.

Pages 40-41
A mirror may be useful. Look back through the book and keep your eyes peeled. Vital information could be lurking anywhere.

Answers

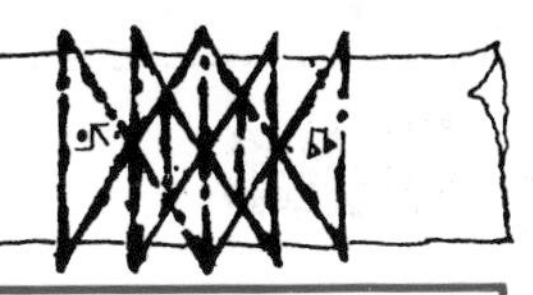

Page 4

Zoonal's route is marked in red.

Page 5

Hercula's route is marked in black.

Page 6

At first glance, the map seems useless, but when Waldo reads Balonius's diary, he realizes that most of the writing is in Turtelese, a language identical to our own but with each word and number written backwards. Translated, the Turtelese inscription on the map plate says:

The Nachos Region
Draw two lines from the summits of the four highest mountains. On the point where they cross lies El Taco.
12 arms = 1 leg

The four highest mountains are the Heights of Sloth (11 legs), Mount Guacamole (10.1 legs), Jaguar Crest (9.7 legs) and Mount Macaw (9.5 legs). When Waldo draws two lines from their summits, they cross just below Toucan Crest.

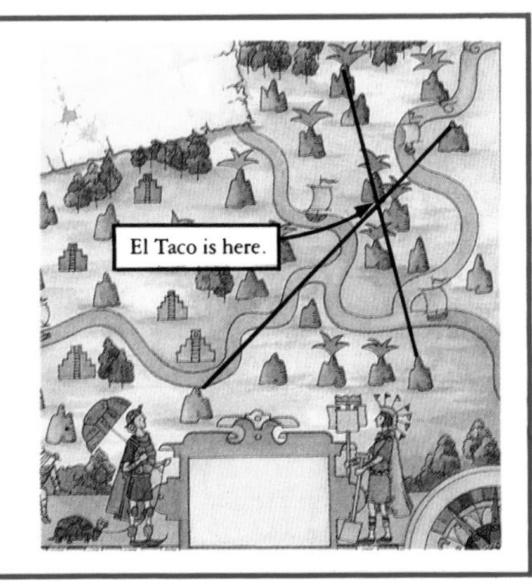

Page 7

Sir Gelfrid and Hildegarde locate Lollo Rosso City by a process of elimination. From clue 5, they know that Lollo Rosso City is due south east of Loen City. This means it could be C, D, or G.
If Lollo Rosso City is C, then Loen City must be A. According to clues 1 and 2, Crocodopolis City lies east of Twystia City and south east of Groen City. This means Crocodopolis City can only be D or G. If it is D then Twystia City must be C and Groen City, B. If it is G, then Twystia City can be either E or F and Groen City, A or C. But in each of these cases, Twystia's or Groen's place is occupied by either Lollo Rosso or Loen City, so Lollo Rosso City cannot be C.
If Lollo Rosso City is D, then Loen City must be B. The cities of Crocodopolis, Twystia and Groen can be located at G, at E or F, and at A or C respectively. But this leaves no position free for Mythika City, which lies east of Desperanda City according to clue 3.
This leaves G as the only solution. If Lollo Rosso City is G, then the cities of Crocodopolis, Twystia and Groen are D, C and B respectively. Loen City is A, and Mythika City and Desperanda City are F and E.

Page 8

Agent Mistral's rendezvous is at Compass Square. This is the ninth of the 12 stations between Via Sinistra and Kriptovia Square and is open at midday.

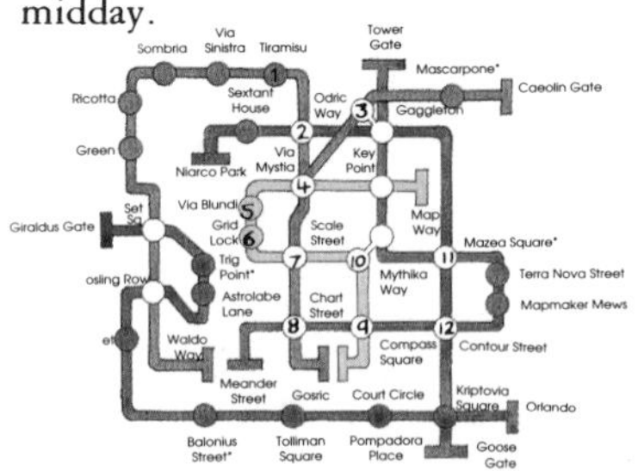

Page 9

These are the seven moves of the Deadly Dance:

1 Hercula moves from A to E
2 Thrumos moves from C to G to A
3 Dogbeast 1 moves from H to D to C to G
4 Dogbeast 2 moves from F to B to H to D to C
5 Hercula moves from E to F to B to H
6 Thrumos moves from A to E to F
7 Dogbeast 1 moves from G to A

Page 10

Waldo decodes the message using the cipher wheel on Orlando Bombasto's locket case. The arrow on the wheel is pointing at A and B. Looking at the message, Waldo realizes that each letter has been substituted by its following letter, so that A becomes B, B becomes C and so on. Decoded, the message says:

The Turquoise Amulet of Twitta is buried under the tree due south of the place where the northernmost of the six statues once stood.

According to the inscription on the plan, none of the six statues stood in vertical, horizontal or diagonal line with any of the others. By a process of elimination, Waldo finds the positions of the four missing statues. These are marked in black. Once he realizes that the plan is pointing west, it is easy to locate the lost amulet.

The amulet is buried here.

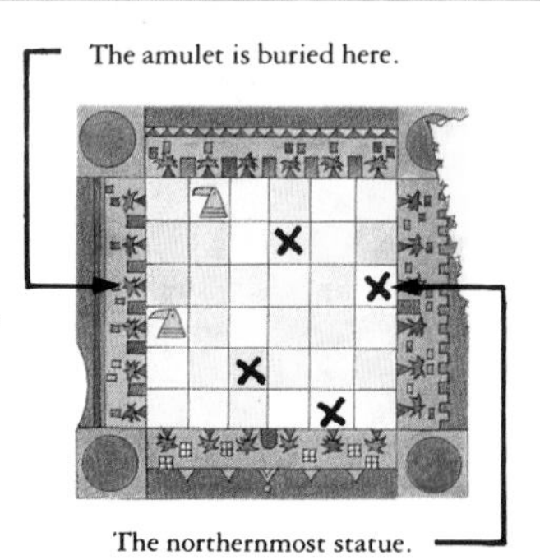

The northernmost statue.

Page 11

Mistral's route to the message drop is marked in black.

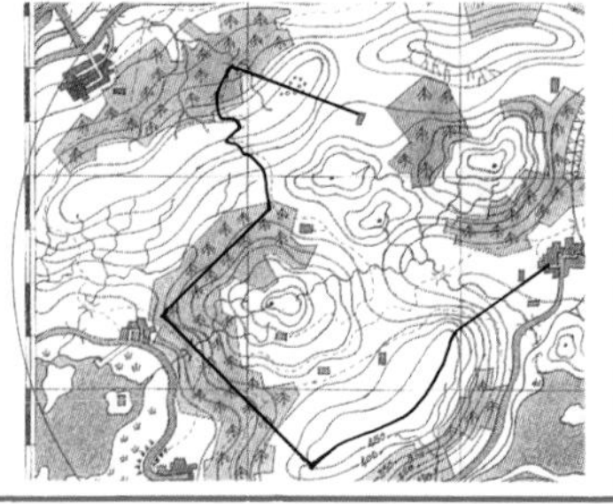

Pages 12-13

Hercula finds the three secret symbols of Ar using a process of elimination. The symbols in their correct order are

▽ ⌂ ʍʍ

Her route to the Crocodile Crown is marked in black.

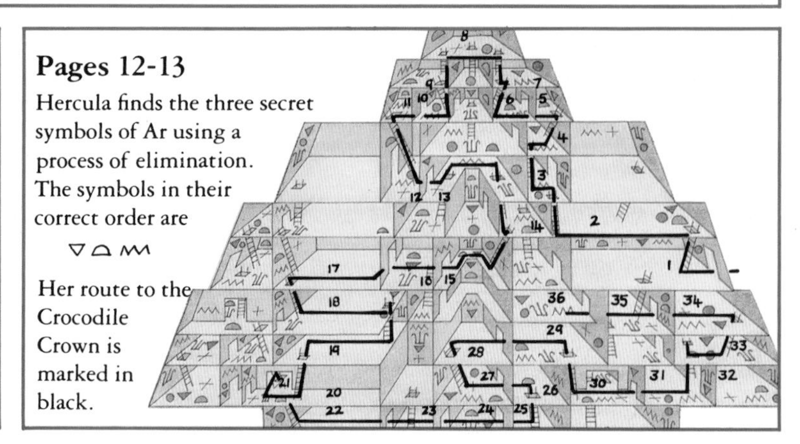

Pages 14-15

Sir Gelfrid and Hildegarde locate their cell and the knights' dungeon by matching the turrets in the picture with those on the plan. The matching turrets are marked with asterisks. The route from the cell to the dungeon is in black, while the route from the dungeon to the safe hall door is in red.

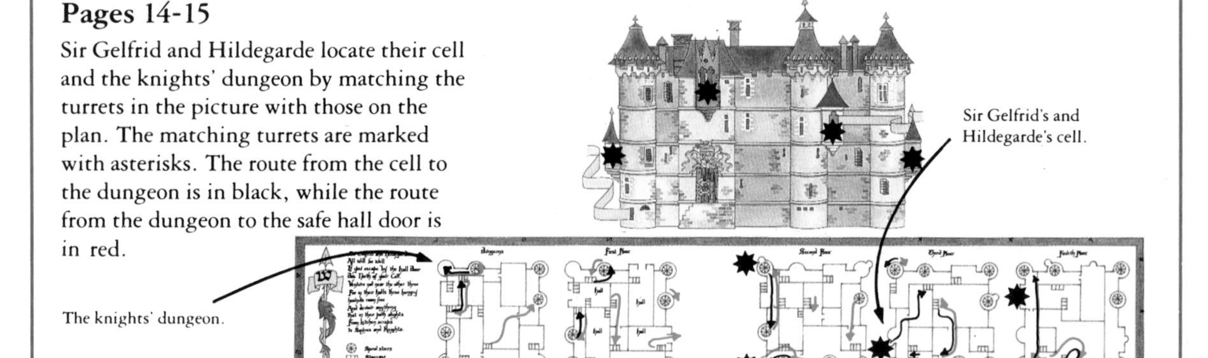

The knights' dungeon.

Sir Gelfrid's and Hildegarde's cell.

Pages 16-17

According to Balonius, the Triangulans give directions by describing the destination then listing the corners of the triangle in which it is located. The route is a straight line from Triangula. Waldo finds Triangula on the map by looking for a triangle with a symbol inside and symbols at each corner that match those in the diary. Then he finds the city of the Turtels, using the symbols on the diagram to the left of the map. His route between Triangula and the city of the Turtels is marked in red. The symbols are circled in black.

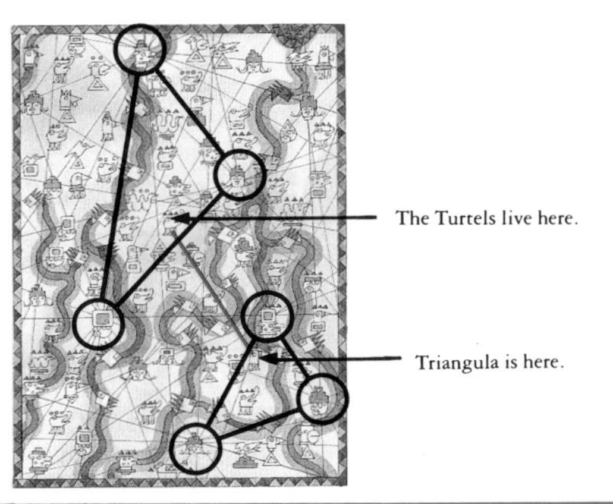

Pages 18-19

The route to the Labyrinka Prison is marked in black.

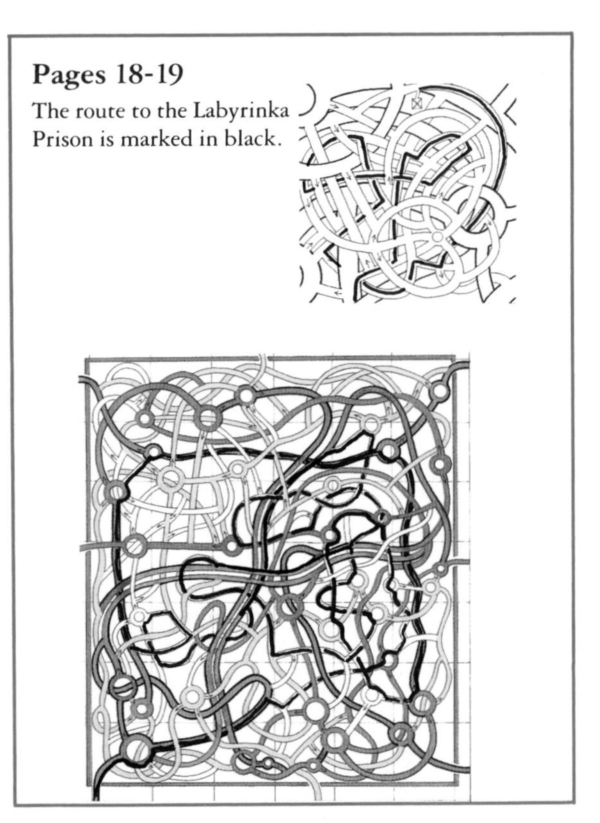

Pages 20-21

First of all, Mistral reads Lucasta's instructions in the correct order. This is what they say:

Walk through three rooms then enter the room with no 'y' in its name and look for the parcel behind the shutter of the third window.

From Cyclone's message, Mistral knows that the layout of the interior of the Casa Fantasa has remained unchanged for 300 years, but the exterior has been altered. She matches up the paintings with the plan, noting how many windows are on each face of the house, according to the pictures, and which direction the plan is pointing. Then Mistral locates most of the rooms on the plan, using the architect's notes. Finally she follows Lucasta's instructions. They lead her through three rooms, the Grand Entrance Hall, the Great Hall and a room which could be the study or the boudoir, into the music room – a room with no 'y' in its name. In Mistral's time, the music room's large single window has been divided into three smaller windows. The parcel is behind the shutter of the third window. Her route is shown in red.

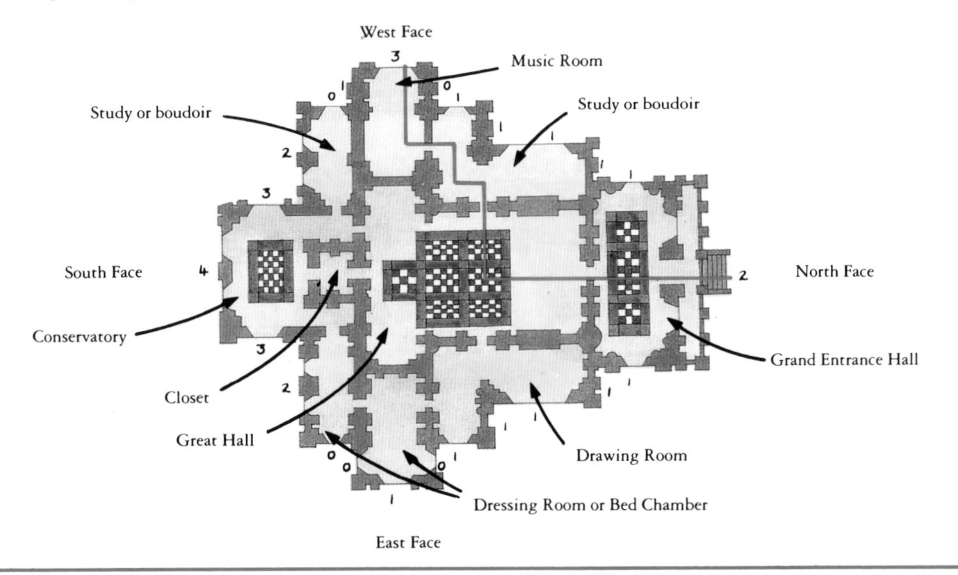

Pages 22-23

Hercula's route is shown in black.

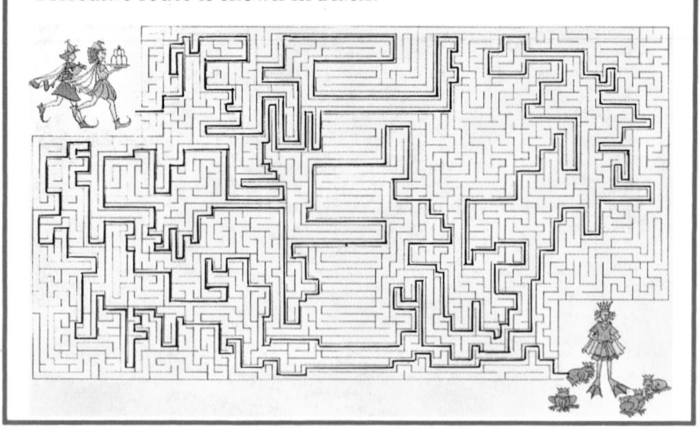

Pages 24-25

Sir Gelfrid's and Hildegarde's route is marked in black. They reach Bombastus's Castle with two surplus geese.

Pages 26-27

From the diary, Waldo learns that Bokonsrikta is deserted during the Pythonic Games except for three guards who have a restricted view of the city from three towers. The streets they can see down are marked in red. Using the description in the diary, Waldo locates the Temple of Pythonia on the plan, then traces the diarist's route to the temple. He remembers that it crossed streets within view of the towers on 11 occasions, when the guards' backs were turned. Once he has escaped from the temple, using the skeleton key, he must retrace this route, marked in black, out of the city.

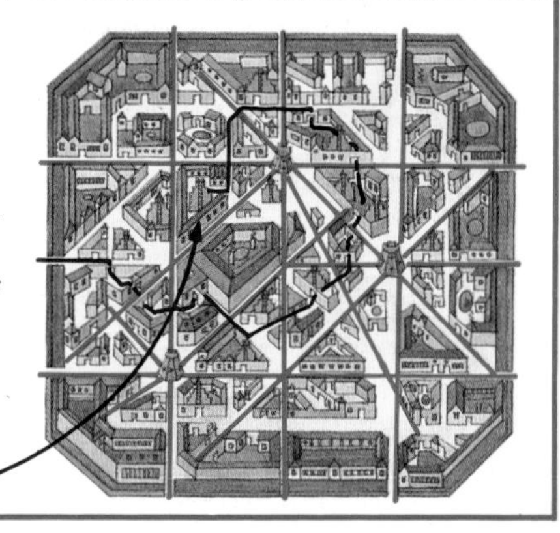

The Temple of Pythonia.

Pages 28-29

Luckily Gidius's directions are easy to translate. In Gmegiddion, all words beginning with a vowel or a consonant, such as F, H, or L, that sounds like a vowel when said out loud, start with "g". All other words start with "gy". The route is marked in black.

Gidius's chest is buried here.

Pages 30-31

To find the Elite Gang's mystery destination, Mistral puts the airline tickets into their correct order. From Lucasta's letter, she knows that the first airport, Ricotta, is in Mascarpone, the location of the Casa Fantasa (see page 20). Then she finds the Elite Gang's route on the flight chart. This is marked in black and leads to Sombria. Mistral can take a shorter route, shown in red, via Cassata.

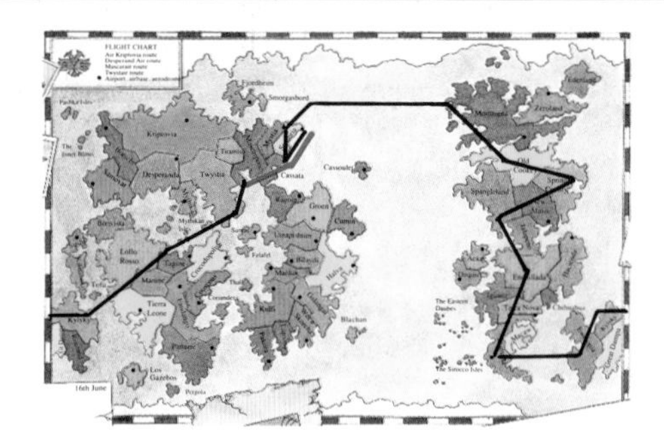

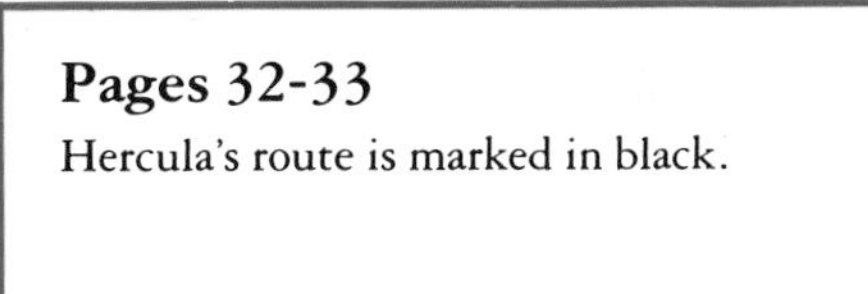

Pages 32-33

Hercula's route is marked in black.

The Hypokondryad's cave.

Pages 34-35

Sir Gelfrid and Hildegarde realize that the Path Perilous can only cross each line of squares headed by a 1 once, so they make sure that they tread on every square of the Path in the previous rows or columns before they cross these lines.
The first part of the Path is easy to find. It goes along the first seven squares in row 7 then up column 7 through two rows headed 1 to row 4.
The Path can't go up to row 2 then down to row 4 as it would need to go up through row 2 for a third time to reach the rows above, so the duo deduce that it must go along four squares in row 4 to column 4.

From there, the Path must pass through the three columns to the left before it can cross column 4 for a third time and go to column 5. First it moves one square to the left into the next column, also a 4, then it goes up just one square to row 6.
From there it can only travel left through column 3 to column 4 and then up through row 3 to row 7. Now all four squares in column 4 have been crossed.
Next the Path goes along row 7, completing its passage through columns 3,4 and 4 until it reaches column 5. As only two squares have been crossed in this column, Gelfrid and Hildegarde figure out that the Path must go down through three squares to row 6. To complete row 6, the Path passes through three squares to column 7. Finally, the Path leads up three squares to row 7 and across into column 1 to the Singing Rock.

Pages 36-37

Waldo locates Chirpeecheep and El Taco using the Cheeps' directions and the strange compass. As the symbol in the red box at the bottom of the map matches one of the symbols on the compass, Waldo correctly assumes that it shows the direction the map is pointing. Then he finds the towns using the diagonal lines on each town symbol to calculate his bearings. Now he can plot his route. This is shown in black and the matching pairs of tunnels are numbered in order.

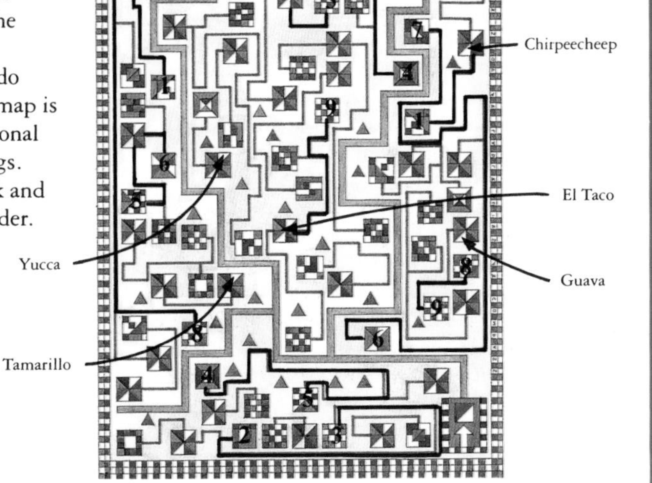

Pages 38-39

Gidius's secret landing route is marked in black.

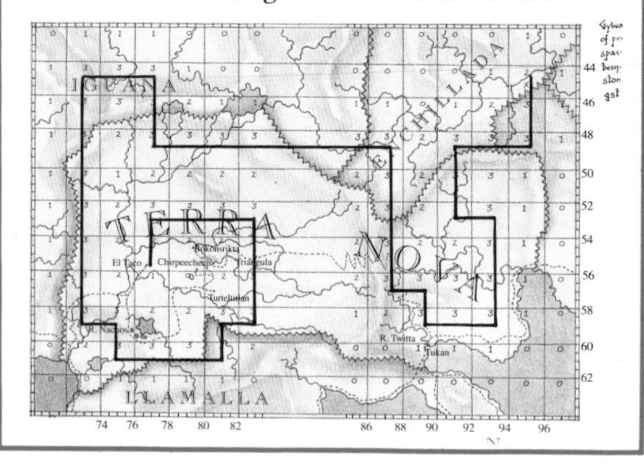

Pages 40-41

Look for the answer elsewhere in this section.

The Strange Story of the Stone

Can you unravel the tangled tale of the stone? All the information lies hidden in the book. Here are some useful hints to point you in the right direction.

- **6** Where do the people on the map come from?
- **7** Mappa Blundi could be useful later on.
- **8** Read the documents carefully. Do some of the names sound familiar? Can you identify a thief? What could the "stone operation" be? Maybe this will make more sense later on.
- **10** Orlando Bombasto – Lucasta's ancestor?
- **18-19** Did you read the Declaration? Why is Teri Firma wearing a strange headdress?
- **20-21** Lucasta seems very interested in the Dark Ages. Do you recognize the symbol above the plan's title?
- **24-25** Does the name "Bombastus" ring any bells?
- **26-27** Have you read the letter? Does anything jog your memory? Can you spot a familiar face?
- **30-31** Did you notice the newspaper clipping? The flight chart is worth studying too. Is there a country missing? What is Lucasta's destination?
- **32-33** Where does Tikitaka come from? Take a good look at the jewel.
- **34-35** Have you seen the rock before?
- **36-37** Did you notice Waldo's new outfit?
- **38-39** Where will the trio land? Which time zone have they entered?

And Finally . . .

Did you notice:

. . . where Twystia City is on Mappa Blundi? The Twystians believed that their city was in the middle of the Dark Age world. A thousand years earlier, the Mythikan Deities located Harmonika, the heart of early Mythikan civilization, in the middle of their map of the world. Both the Twystians and the Mythikan gods wrongly assumed that the world was flat.

. . . the rivers and some of the places on Balonius's map (page 6), the Triangulan chart (page 17) and the carpet map (page 37) can be matched up with those on the map of Terra Nova (pages 38-39)?

. . . the objects found with the map of Terra Nova? After a long trek through the tunnels of the Nachos Region, Waldo finally reached El Taco where he received a warm welcome and lived happily ever after.

. . . the swagglebird feathers on Lucasta's hat? Orlando Bombasto returned from Terra Nova with a shipload of swagglebirds and made his fortune by selling their bright blue feathers for hats and fans. He then married Marco Niarco's daughter, Sarcasta, and built the Casa Fantasa. As the centuries passed, the poor swagglebirds became rarer and rarer. These gentle fowl, of whom one acted as Vaeralyn's messenger, are now extinct.

. . . the goosey names on Mistral's hiking map? Geese have been held in high esteem in Twystia since the dawn of civilization. The Blue Goose is Twystia's national symbol.

. . . the wavy line on the Twystian metro ticket (page 8) reappears on the Zarkan crest (page 18)? Could the Twystians be the Zarkans' ancestors?

. . . the towers on Mistral's hiking map? These are where the Twystian cartographers lived in accordance with their vows of silence, solitude and secrecy. These eccentric mapmakers left their latest charts in chests outside the towers for lost wayfarers to consult.

. . . the lyre on Balonius's map? When Tikitaka sailed to Harmonika, one of his crew, a Turtel, brought along his lyre. The admiring islanders promptly adopted it as their national instrument.

. . . the stepped pyramid of Ar? This was copied from Tikitaka's drawing of a Terra Novan temple.

. . . if Lucasta found the stone? The Terra Novan Secret Service suspected that this "stone" was none other than the long lost Crystal of Leyheyhey, given to the El Tackans at the dawn of time to protect Quirk from Zarkan attack. They hoped that Lucasta would lead Agent Mistral to the crystal, which would then be returned to El Taco to perform its vital role.

First published in 1993 by Usborne Publishing Ltd,
Usborne House, 83-85 Saffron Hill, London
EC1N 8RT, England.

Universal Edition

Printed in Spain. First published in America August 1993